Joseph's Devil - The Joseph Series –
Part Two

By Denzil Lloyd Wallace

Contents

Preface

So, this is my second book, and I still do not consider myself a writer. However, I do enjoy writing. I love creating ideas and putting them on paper. So I decided to keep the ball rolling and write Joseph's Devil. Joseph's Devil is a continuation to Joseph's Angel of my imagination of what the spiritual realm, (both good and bad) might be like. Similar to Joseph's Angel, there are angels and demons. This time, the story is told through the lens of a demon named Krimion, as he tries to conquer the soul of Joseph Johnson.

Just like Joseph's Angel, the scenes in this book are not necessarily biblical. So any Christian reading this book should take all scenes with a grain of salt. Consider this book entertainment, with a sprinkle of biblical similarities.

Also, this book is not intended to convert non-believers into Christians either. However, if you do become converted, I won't be mad one bit.

Lastly, I want to give a special thanks to my wife, Nichole. Even though she has a medical condition that limits her at times, she's still the glue to our family. Thank you for your support on this project.

Now to all you readers, enjoy Joseph's Devil.

His Perspective

"I used to love Jehovah. He communicated daily with me about his affairs and plans. I loved and served him gladly. I praised him constantly. Jehovah took me all over the galaxies. He showed me the various planets he created and the multiple solar systems in space. I was amazed at his craftiness. How did he know how to create planets, suns, moons, and stars? He taught me so much. And I was eager to learn more. I wanted him to show me everything. I wasn't jealous of his power; I just wanted to see and know everything he knows."

"As mentioned before, he showed me the many galaxies out in space. There was one particular universe that he wouldn't give me access. I said to him, Lord, what occupies that Universe to the North of your throne? His reply: *"You can't know about that universe right now, perhaps in the future, you may know."*

"Now, I didn't complain or cry like a spoiled child. I said 'Yes Master', and gladly continued my benevolence to him."

"About 50,000 earth years pass by. I again ask Jehovah about this unknown universe. And once again I am denied. But I continue to serve him. Millions of years then pass by, and he creates Earth. I assumed that he was going to give me this planet to rule. Instead, he gave it to humans. He made man in his image and gave them dominion

5

over all the animals and all the earth. He even commanded these humans to be fruitful and multiply."

"Imagine how I felt, not given a planet to rule, not given the opportunity to reproduce. It was at that moment that I had enough. I, Lucifer, gathered my best angels, packed up our belongings and attempted to move to that Northern Universe that God denied me time and time again."

"It was I, along with you, oh loyal Sansar, who assembled to go to this place and make it our new home. I was to be your leader. I was to be your king. I would have ruled with love and compassion; similar to our Lord. But no, great Jehovah once again denied me access. And instead of having mercy on me, he cast me down to Earth with all the other angels who followed me. Not to rule it, but to wander through it in the invisible realm and watch these ugly, unappreciative, dust-originating, human beings, destroy this beautiful earth that their had God created."

"When those faithful to Jehovah fought us in our revolt, God's number two, Michael, did a horrific thing when he cut off your head. He cemented your feet in tar. It was part of your punishment for siding with me in this revolt. So I do feel as though I owe you the same loyalty that you gave me thousands of years ago. However, I wouldn't be Satan if I was a loyal subject now, would I?"

"And since the day we were cast down to this planet, I've made it my mission to tarnish the name and lives of all humans. Now Sansar, you have been my most faithful servant for all of these years. You have been successful in destroying the lives of many millions of humans.

Great men and women of God fell for our deceptions and let sin sever their relationship with God."

"But then Jesus came to Earth and ruined everything! He defeated death because he is God. He raised up the souls of many that were dead and brought them back up to paradise. But we didn't let that stop us, right Sansar? We continued to have our ways with the humans. Yes, some remained faithful to God, but we have our list of mighty men of God who fell by the wayside. bishops, pastors, preachers, teachers, those who performed miracles in the name of Jesus, and those who cast out demons. Some of these great men have we brought over to the dark side. Through sex, through drugs, through hatred and violence, have I kept sin in the hearts of many of God's children.

"So now Sansar, aside from me, you are the most conniving demon in all the universe. By yourself have you brought down powerful people. kings, queens, presidents, lawyers, judges, to name a few. So I am a little perplexed at the fact that it has been eight years and you still have not been able to bring me Joseph. I warned you that failure to bring me this person would be catastrophic for you."

"Satan, please release these chains from my hands and feet. I know I was given eight years to hand you Joseph, but can't we face the fact that he is one of God's chosen and is destined to reign with Christ when he returns? Undoubtedly my failure with Joseph cannot overshadow my successes with the others I've brought to you.

"Sansar, Sansar, Sansar; this is not the agreement we made eight years ago. I've watched some of the tricks you've tried to play on Joseph. You've tried sex; that didn't work. You've tried drugs; that didn't work. You've tried financial hardship; that didn't work. You've tried lies

7

and deceit by his friends and family, and that didn't work. I thought you would have known by now that Joseph is too spiritually mature for these weak tricks. Now I think it's time for you to receive your reward for your failure with the Joseph Johnson project."

Satan then calls for his guards.

"Lorencio, Domingo, feed Sansar to the A-hounds!"

The A-hounds are 100 four-footed Wolf-like angelic pets. These pets were assistants of Satan and his warriors in their attempt to move to the universe above God's throne. They were cast down with Satan and his fallen angels onto earth. These pets are not loving house pets like your average cat or dog. Since having been cast out of heaven, they are hungry for food. They feed on the souls of un-saved non-believers. But after a while, those lost souls lose their taste, and the hounds become hungry again. They are so hungry that Satan has to keep them locked away in a dungeon to keep them away from him or the other demons. Now Satan is about to feed Sansar to these hounds.

"Please My Lord," begs Sansar. "You don't have to do this."

"Don't tell me what you think I don't have to do. I know that I don't have to do this; I want to do this. I want to hear you scream in agony as the hounds masticate on all over your headless soul."

"Yes, my Lord. My headless soul. My head that was lost while fighting for you and for what you believed. This is the thanks I get, Satan? I have been by your side every step of the way. Certainly, you can be as faithful to me as I have been to you?"

"Sansar, you're such an idiot! If I wasn't faithful to God almighty, millions of years ago, what makes you think that I would be faithful to you? Seriously, Sansar? The only person I am loyal to is myself. Well, I've had enough of the chit-chatter. Guards, throw him in the dungeon!"

Lorencio and Domingo grab Sansar by the hands and feet and start dragging him toward the dungeon. Even bound by chains, Sansar is still stronger than the two demons and is actively denying their attempt to cast him to the hounds. Sansar's hands are chained together; the same can be said of his feet. He uses his chained up arms like a baseball bat, and swings it at Domingo; hitting Domingo square on the head. Then, like a bull running toward a Matador, Lorencio lunges at Sansar but is unable to strike Sansar because of Sansar's feline reflexes. Sansar continues to dance around the room, dodging and evading the two guards. At the same time, he is trying to talk Satan out of his decision.

"Please my master, my lord, and my King. Save me from this moment of torment. I won't let you down again."

Satan ignores Sansar's plea for clemency. He's entertained and at the same time annoyed with Domingo and Lorencio's inability to take hold of Sansar.

Domingo and Lorencio chase after Sansar throughout the room. They finally trap him in a corner. Slowly they approach him, as they are frightened by his power. They prepare once more to take hold of him. But right before they make another attack at Sansar, Satan steps in, and with one clean sweep of his right hand, he knocks Lorencio and Domingo to the ground. Satan grabs hold of the weaker Sansar, picks Sansar up by his two feet, and begins to continuously and viciously slam Sansar to the ground. When he is done, Satan opens the door to the dungeon ever so slightly, so that the A-Hounds could not escape. He throws Sansar down into the cell and watches as the A-Hounds feast on their latest meal.

Sansar is in excruciating pain. Screaming from the piercing bites of the Hounds, they are ripping apart his very soul. But because he is a spirit being, and will not be permanently killed until the return of Christ, his soul will not decay or die. Unless Satan releases Sansar from the dungeon, Sansar will be experiencing a lifetime of torture.

Satan walks over to his throne and calls for all of his underlings.

Before him stands 10 million fallen angels. Now known as demons or devils, these fallen angels assist Satan in terminating the lives of mankind.

"Now listen carefully, every one of you! Sansar was my right-hand assistant. He's done more for me than all of you in here combined. But as you can see, I have thrown him in the dungeon for the Hounds to eat. I want each one of you to see what can be your fate if you fail to produce the results I demand."

Pointing to one of his subjects, he calls to him; "Manford?"

"Yes, your Majesty."

"Remind us all of our slogan please?"

"As many Christians left behind, sir."

"Well stated, Manford. Our only goal while on this horrible planet is to ensure that as many humans as possible, especially Christians, are left behind when Jesus comes and raptures the church.

10

Now, I have been in pursuit of Joseph Johnson from the time I heard of his foretold calling. 27 years ago, while Sansar was tormenting a Christian, he overheard a heavenly angel speaking to the mother of Joseph. The angel informed her that she was pregnant and that the child would be an anointed child of God, called into ministry. "

"When Sansar reported this to me, I immediately called for the death of this child. But Jehovah would not allow me to harm the unborn child. He stated that I may begin to test and tempt the child when the child turns thirteen years old. So from the age of thirteen, I assigned Sansar to tempt JJ periodically. But JJ was focused on his God. For a teenager, he was well-disciplined in godly behavior. Nevertheless, I knew it was a matter of time before his sexual hormones would kick in. That, along with peer-pressure, would surely bring him to fornicate. It took a little longer than I would have hoped. The stupid boy was afraid to talk to girls. Even though he had a major crush on this girl named Karen, he was never bold enough to flirt with her and try to get in-between her panties."

"But Sansar was relentless with his chase of Joseph. His perseverance finally paid off when at the age of 19, Sansar got JJ to have a threesome with two other girls, have sex with another girl in the basement of his church, and have sex with the now married Karen. All this happened within a matter of a week."

"I was so proud of Sansar. We were close to achieving our goal with JJ. But that was not to be as God somehow pulled him back into his graces. Joseph is now spiritually stronger and wiser than ever before."

11

"Now my hands are tied with other human beings that I am dealing with personally. I need a volunteer to replace Sansar on this Joseph project. But before anyone opts into this assignment, realize that if you fail to deliver Joseph to me promptly, your fate will be the same as your predecessor, Sansar. So, which of you will take on this challenge?

Immediately and without hesitation, responds a demon named Krimion.

"I'll do it, my Lord. I will take on Joseph Johnson. I have been observing him from a distance and I know what it takes to bring him to fall."

Krimion is an up and coming demon. He has moved up within the ranks of Satan's army. He has a plethora of humans on his resume of whom he has caused to fall from God's grace. American presidents, famous sports athletes, well-known actors, and a variety of European and African leaders are among his list of conquests.

Krimion is not next in line after Sansar. Julian and Issachar were 3rd and 4th in leadership. They wanted no part of the Joseph project, therefore they kept their mouths shut.

Satan now elevates above his herd of demons. He's quite the alluring creature. Hovering over his people, his beauty shines throughout the room. The former son of morning star still has his glow. Shining in white; the radiance of his brightness causes his people to bow their heads in admiration and fear. Only Jehovah can best his beauty.

"Alright, Krimion," Satan replies. I suppose it is your turn. You do seem up to the task. Your hatred for God and everything he stands for is almost as great as mine. I'll give you five years to bring me Joseph. If you fail, you'll meet your doom in the dungeon with Sansar."

Krimion bows before his master and walks away to prepare for his takeover attempt of Mr. Joseph Johnson.

On His Own
Place - Heaven

"Gather around children. I have a story for you all. Something many of you has been wondering about. First, let me say, that I used to love Lucifer. Still do, in fact. After all, he's my first created being. Imagine, that before any of you were created, I created him. I would take him with me to visit all of the planets of all the galaxies I've created. Lucifer is an intelligent being. He caught on well to everything I taught him. Inquisitive, he was. He never stopped asking me questions. And for the most part, I answered his questions. However, there was one question that I never answered for him."

"As many of you know, there is a realm above heaven that I have blocked off from anyone's access. It's another universe that is in preservation. Lucifer wanted access to this universe, but I would not grant him access whenever he would ask. It's not like I wasn't going to grant him access eventually. It just wasn't the right time."

"As time went on, Lucifer, along with many other angels, including some of you standing here today, witnessed my creation of Earth. For some reason, Lucifer thought that I was going to anoint him king of Earth and all the humans. I never gave him any reason to think so, but he had his own dreams and aspirations that he never informed me of, even though I knew his thoughts and desires."

"He became invidious over the humans; especially their ability to populate the earth with their offspring. He felt that the humans were lesser beings than was he. So after realizing that Earth was not for him, he asked me again to see the universe from above. Again, I told him that I would give him access sometime in the future. Well as you can imagine, he didn't take well my retort. So he decided to take matters into his own hands. Lucifer is quite the persuader. He convinced about a third of the angels I had at that time, to join forces with him and escape into the unknown world."

"Of course, I thwarted those plans and had an unfortunate all-out war with him and his followers. Many of you helped me to defeat him. And as punishment for his treason, and to also add insult to injury, I cast Lucifer and his followers to Earth. Some fallen angels are in the uttermost parts of the earth, bound into chains. Others, like Satan, can roam free, but without full access to what Earth has to offer."

"Satan then introduced sin to the humans. I won't get into a history lesson on this, as you all know it very well. His desire to bring devastation to the human race has been his ambition since he was cast down. And to a certain degree, he has been successful."

"If you recall, about eight years ago, I sent Gardéus down to earth to monitor a man by the name of Joseph Johnson. Satan assigned

14

Sansar, his Chief Lieutenant, to lure Joseph into sin. Sansar did succeed, but he wasn't able to bring Joseph down enough to the point where he lost his salvation. Gardéus was somewhat influential with Joseph's victory over sin. And once I realized that Joseph was spiritually strong enough to go on without Gardéus, I moved Gardéus on to other projects."

"Over the succeeding eight years, Satan demanded that Sansar bring Joseph down to hell, but Sansar was unsuccessful and has been punished harshly by Satan."

"As of a few minutes ago, Satan has assigned a younger, stronger, and more determined demon to go after Joseph. His plans are even more wicked and demented than that of Sansar's."

"Should I summon Gardéus from his current mission so that he may go back to Joseph?" Suggests Michael.

"No, that won't be necessary," responds the Lord. "Joseph is going to have to handle this one on his own. Let's see how much faith and trust in me he really has. Joseph has been doing pretty well over the last eight years, but trouble is on the horizon. This new demon has some tricks up his sleeve that Joseph is not used to. Time will tell how he fares."

"Which demon has taken on the assignment now," asks Faila?

"It's Krimion. And we are well aware of the damage he's done on behalf of Satan."

"Oh no," cries Jaime! "Sansar was bad, but Krimion is worse. He's so militant in his approach to the humans. I'll never forget the way he influenced Hitler. Oh, Great Jehovah, how do you plan to assist Joseph with this demon?"

"Well, Joseph is still responsible for his own actions. Krimion can only do but so much. The power is in Joseph's hands. Krimion might cause chaos around Joseph, but it's up to Joseph on how he reacts. So for now, we're all going to keep our distance. We'll intercede, if necessary."

The host of angels cannot believe that God is going to leave Joseph to fend for himself against the brutish attacks of Krimion. Many of them start to whisper among each other, in concern for the young preacher.

But God knew their thoughts. "Remember guys; my Spirit is still with Joseph. All he has to do is rely on me for guidance, and all will be well."

The Pastor

Years have passed, and Joseph Johnson has come a long way in his ministry. Seven months after realizing his purpose in ministry, Joseph started his first church in the Bed-Stuy section of Brooklyn, New York. This was of course, with the blessing of his former Pastor, Bishop David Alexander.

Bishop Alexander was extremely fond of Joseph and was delighted when Joseph married the bishop's daughter, Willow. Yes indeed, Joseph married Willow seven years ago, after courting her for one year. Willow was the perfect match for Joseph. She carried herself with dignity and class. She spoke proper English and annunciated every word appropriately. Still, she isn't conceited, even though she is well educated. A first-rate chef who makes an excellent fillet Minot.

Not only does Willow have these delightful traits, but she is also a sight of beauty. Drop dead gorgeous! At 5 feet 8 inches, and 165 pounds, this African American goddess has dark chocolate skin, full luscious lips, and big wide-eyed brown eyes. For the past three years, she has had her hair in a natural look. Joseph loved the way black women looked with their hair natural; not that he had something against women who had perms or weaves, but a natural-hair-looking woman always drew his attention.

Like many women before, Willow had a serious crush on Joseph during her teen and early adult years. Joseph had a thing for her as well, back in the day, but he was too shy to approach her, and Willow was not the type to make the first move toward a guy, especially in her teen years.

It wasn't until after his encounter with God that he began to pray for a spouse. After several months of searching, he found himself in love with Willow, and they started dating. Once the church members found out that they were dating, talks of a wedding spread throughout the congregation. All the single women were envious of Willow. After all, Joseph was on the single ladies most wanted list.

The two of them got married on a cool spring afternoon in the month of May. It was a small wedding, with only 50 guests. Immediate family and friends attended. After the wedding, they went on a European cruise and visited countries like France and Italy. They were even able to visit the Vatican, home of the Pope. Joseph was amazed at the beauty of the historic landmark and he took many pictures.

Upon returning to New York from their honeymoon, Joseph started his church. Initially, Willow did not like the idea of being the wife of a Pastor. She did not like the idea of sharing Joseph's time between herself and the needs of the church. But she eventually gave in when she realized that pastoring was something Joseph was born to do.

Bishop Alexander volunteered to donate five hundred thousand dollars and fifty of his members to Joseph's ministry. But Joseph turned down this gracious act of the bishop. Joseph wanted to start from scratch. He wanted to bring in unbelievers, drug addicts, gang members, and prostitutes into his church. He did not wish to have a building filled with already saved folks.

Joseph had a strategy on how to build church membership. If Joseph weren't a preacher, he would have been a politician. His motto was, '*the proof is in the pudding.*' He planned to do good things for the people of the community and in turn, they would give back to his cause.

Before he ever had a building for his church, he started preaching on the street corners. One day, while preaching, a homeless man with hardly any clothes on his back, begged Joseph for some money. Joseph gave the man fifty bucks, a place to stay in his home, and assistance in finding employment. This homeless man is now a self-sufficient contributor to society and a deacon in Joseph's church.

On another occasion, Joseph gave out clothes and toys for children. This wasn't uncommon for Christians to do during Christmas season, but Joseph was doing this during the month of June.

In addition to these acts, he would talk to any and everybody who was willing to engage in conversation. Whether it was religion, politics, or sports, Joseph liked the idea of sharing his views as well as listening to the opinions of others.

Over time, Joseph became a respectable man within the community. Everyone knew his name. Once his name became common among the people, he decided it was time to start his church.

There was a commercial property available for rent. It was once a hardware store that had gone out of business. The owner was Mr. Resnick, a Jewish man. He formerly lived in Israel, but in 1975 he moved to the states to avoid the never-ending conflict between the Israelis and Palestinians.

Mr. Resnick came to the states believing in that American dream. The dream that you can be successful with hard work and determination. When he first moved to the states, Mr. Resnick worked odd jobs for several years while living at home with his parents. His parents didn't charge him rent. That allowed him to save his money in order to get his own apartment or to start a business. He quickly found a money-maker in the field of Real Estate.

From 1975 to 1980, Mr. Resnick saved enough money to purchase several pieces of property within the borough of Brooklyn. Much of these properties he would rent out, while others he would refurbish and sell for almost twice the original purchase price.

19

He turned himself into a wealthy man, but you would never know of his wealth by the way he carried himself. He recycles the same five pairs of slacks every week, wore a white, black or gray shirt, and the most conventional looking white pair of sneakers. He never cared much for clothes - still doesn't to this day. His wife, Rita, has to force him to buy a new pair of pants if a current pair is getting worn out. He pretty much looked like that uncool nerd in school that no one gave any attention. He barely groomed his hair, and he wasn't much of a talker either.

Mr. Resnick knew about Joseph's good deeds in the community and agreed to rent him the property at a discounted but fair market rate. He even provided Joseph with laborers to help Joseph build the church.

Mr. Resnick is a devout Jew, so Joseph was a bit perplexed with his generosity to a Christian cause.

Mr. Resnick could sense that Joseph was confused by his kindness.

"You know what, Joseph? You and I serve the same God. The Christian origins stem from the Torah. Jews believe in one God. Christians believe in one God. The only difference is that most Jews do not believe that Jesus is the Messiah. But whether he is or isn't the Messiah doesn't change the fact that we both serve the same God, the God of Abraham, Isaac, and Jacob. The God of the twelve tribes of Israel. So any person who serves this God is a brother of mine. And any brother of mine in need is a brother I am willing to help. Besides, we Jews are still waiting for the Messiah to come. Maybe your Jesus is the

Messiah. What do we really know?" he asks in a somewhat mystified manner.

Joseph was astonished. He had never heard a person who practiced Judaism speak like this before.

"Well, you know what, Mr. Resnick?"

"Please, we are friends. Call me Alex."

"Okay, Alex. I like how your mind works. If more men thought like you, the world would be a better place."

So with the help of Alex and his men, Joseph's church was up and running within two weeks.

Once the neighborhood saw that Joseph Johnson was the pastor of the new store-front church, many of them flocked to his Sunday services.

Months went by and Sunday after Sunday, membership increased. After two months of services, the church had 105 full-fledged members.

The building had an occupancy of 120 people. Often there was standing room only, with as many as 170 people in the room. The sanctuary was crowded and uncomfortable.

"We need a bigger building," shouts one of the new members.

"Sure, we can get a new building," responds Joseph. But it has to be in this neighborhood. I'll contact a real estate agent, and see what I can find. In the meantime, I'm going to ask if we can pool our money together to help fund our new location. Please, please, do not sell your

21

houses, use your rent money, or dip into your retirement! Give what you realistically can, and God will provide the rest."

Joseph put Rich Tatum, one of his first members, in charge of the church's building fund project. Rich is the owner of a welding company. He immediately gathered many of the members together to organize ways to raise money for their new building.

Joseph found a building for sale just seven blocks away from their current location.

"This building is too big and costs too much," he thinks to himself.

The building was indeed enormous and high in value. It was an old manufacturing building. Very spacious.

"This building could probably fit about 20,000 people. I don't have 20,000 members."

It was at that moment that Joseph heard the voice of the Lord speaking to him, clear as day.

"Joseph, you're wrong. The building is too small. Think bigger."

Although Joseph knew that it was God's voice speaking to him, he couldn't believe that God wanted him to look for a more significant building. Despite his hesitancy, Joseph continued his search for property or real estate for sale.

Meanwhile, Rich was working with the members on organizing the funds.

"How much money do we need?" One person asked.

"Well, we could get a mid-sized church," responds another member. But I think we can do better. We should raise enough money to start a mega-church. A church where we can do a lot more for the community than just a Sunday Sermon. We could start a daycare, a senior center, an elementary school. Nothing is impossible if we trust in God, pull our resources together, and stay committed."

"Wow, you have big dreams," retorts Rich's wife, Jennifer. Just make sure you run this idea and all other ideas by Pastor Johnson. We don't wanna get ahead of ourselves."

A couple of weeks passed by and Joseph was back at church preparing for his Thursday night bible study. When he arrives, he hands over the month's rent to Alex. They were talking for a bit when Joseph mentioned his congregations' plans.

"So, Alex, I just wanted you to know that this building cannot hold all the members on a given Sunday service. We are currently looking for another building."

That's excellent news, Joseph! You guys are expanding. Congratulations!"

"Thank, Alex. However, there's a slight problem."

"And what's that?"

"I need a big building. A huge building. Something that can seat around fifty-thousand people."

"Wow Pastor Johnson, you're aiming high I see."

"Yes, Alex. I believe that this is what God wants me to do."

23

"Well Joseph, are you familiar with the minor league hockey team, the Brooklyn, rollers?"

"Yes, I am. They play over in the Riley arena, over on Cooper Street."

"Well, the owner has sold the team to a group of investors from Philly. The investors are going to move the team over there. Aside from the occasional concert and circus, the hockey team was the arena's main source of income. I know for a fact that the owners of the arena want to rent or sell the place to another business. Your church would be perfect for the arena."

"Ya think! I need to go to the internet to find the owners and their contact information."

"You don't need to do that, Joseph."

"Why not?

"Because I'm one of the owners."

"Get out of here, Alex. You're kidding, aren't you?"

"No sir, I am not kidding at all. I own 55 percent of the building. My cousin, Jerry owns the other 45 percent. The building is yours if you want. Get your congregation together; we'll meet up, and work out the details for payment."

Joseph could not believe what was happening. God had spoken to him previously about needing a more prominent venue; now the site was provided to him through Mr. Resnick.

"Mr. Resnick, I am speechless right now. You're too kind to me. I'm sure you could turn the building into a mall or sell it to one of those bigtime chain franchises. You would make a killer."

"I'm sure you're right, Joseph, But the retail business is dwindling, It's not as profitable as it once was. Besides, our community needs more safe-havens like your church for the inner-city youth to attend. Some of these kids have no manners. Last summer, a black kid was inside a school bus, opened the window by his seat and yelled out, "heil Hitler" to me. Now if I had called him the N-word, I would have been wrong, right? I'm sure the kid probably isn't all that bad, but a place of worship under your leadership could do wonders for boys like him."

"Oh, I know it will," responds Joseph. "Hopefully, I and others will be able to mentor boys and girls like the one you encountered. I have so many ideas for the new building. I can't wait to work over the details with the member's and whatever construction crew I hire."

"Joseph, you can use my cousin Jerry's constructions crew. We'll only charge you three-fourths of the cost. I believe in you and your vision. You are doing great work for all of Brooklyn. Besides, I can see that the favor of God is upon you. As long as I'm alive, you'll have my support as needed."

So this was the introduction of Joseph's mega-church ministry. Initially, Joseph named his store-front church, the "Jesus Saves Pentecostal Church. But after careful consideration, he realized that this name was too cliché for his liking. Also, he didn't want to only draw people of the Pentecostal denomination. He desired to attract a variety of Christian believers. Growing up in church all his life, Joseph grew weary of the dogmatic doctrinal differences between the numerous Christian sects. The fact that one Christian would judge another Christian based on the fact that one was a Methodist, while the other was a Baptist, really bothered him. He wanted to bring everyone together on the universal principles of the bible. At the same time, he didn't want to classify his church as non-denominational either. To Joseph, the term non-denominational was a denomination in itself. The only label Joseph wanted was Christian. It was then where he came up with the name 'Followers of Christ, Christian Church,' also known as, FOC for followers of Christ.

And so for the next several years, FOC became a staple in the community. Their radio and local cable T.V. shows allowed them to reach a broader audience. Their food pantry was second to none throughout the city.

Sansar tried to destroy Joseph's work, but Joseph always remained focused on pleasing God and not himself. So because of his faithfulness to God, God was still with him and helped him fight off the demonic force.

Seizing Her Birthday
Present day.

Joseph and Willow purchased a house in the Mill Basin section of Brooklyn. Five years ago, today, Willow gave birth to their daughter, Willa. Joseph and Willow are throwing a birthday party for their precious daughter. Willa has as much input on the party planning as her parents. She wanted things done a certain way. When she was four years old, her parents introduced her to the classic cartoon, 'Tom and Jerry.' This cartoon became her favorite and was now the theme of the party. For entertainment, instead of hiring a clown, Willa wanted to sing a few songs. Yes, just like her father, Willa is an exceptional singer for her age.

Her dress for the day, a beautiful turquoise colored dress. Turquoise is Willa's favorite color. And don't be fooled, she knows the difference between turquoise and blue. Joseph and Willa spent days online and inside department stores searching for a turquoise dress. Joseph tried to get her to settle for a plain blue dress, but Willa refused to settle for anything other than turquoise. Eventually, Willa and Joseph found her color dress at a local kid's store, and the relief on Joseph's face was equal to the excitement in Willa's.

The party started at 2:00 p.m. sharp. Many of Willa's school friends, friends from the neighborhood, and friends from the church, showed up with gifts in hands. Parents of the kids were there as well. Everyone headed to the backyard for food and games.

Joseph and Willow were busy in the kitchen preparing Mac and cheese, and barbeque chicken. Willow looks at the time on her phone and realizes that the party was starting and she is still in her bedclothes.

"Joseph, I need to freshen up. Do you think you can handle the food until I get back?"

"Yeah baby, don't worry. I got this," he replies with confidence.

Willow leaves to get herself straightened up. Guests continue to enter the Johnson house. Mr. Gimber, along with his son and

27

daughter just arrived. Willa greets them at the door and shows them the way to the backyard.

"Oh Willa, which way is the restroom?" Mr. Gimber asks.

"We have two," she responds. "But the one down here is not working. Go upstairs and make a left, and you'll see the other bathroom there."

"Thanks, I really have to go. Be right back, kids."

So Willa and her friends go to the backyard to take part in the activities. Willa is having a blast. She's playing tag, hopscotch, and sack-racing. Joseph looks on with Joy, as he watches the pleasure on his daughter's face.

About 45 minutes later, Willow comes down. She is decked out from head to toe. One would have thought that it was her birthday.

"Honey, you look stunning," remarks Joseph. "I'm gonna have something special for you later," he flirts.

"Hey, it's my birthday, chimes Willa. You can give mommy your special gift tomorrow!"

A burst of laughter rings from all the adults in the room.

"What? What's so funny?" Willa asks.

"Oh, nothing, pumpkin," answers her mother. "Just enjoy the party. I think it's time for your cake."

"Oh yeah, you're right mommy. Daddy, get the cake. Mommy, get ready to start the music."

Willa planned to sing a big number during the presentation of her birthday cake. The music starts at a slow pace. Willa stands before the crowd with her legs and feet pressed against the other. Her long turquoise short-sleeved dress blends in perfectly with her dark-brown skin. Her wide smile to the crowd displays her bottom front missing tooth. She has the audience's attention. She starts to sing in a slow melodic pace. The music and words she is singing are familiar, but no one can quite recall the name of the song. As the song continues, the song takes a 5-second pause before the music and pace speed up. The adults now realize the song she is singing. It's 'I'm Every Woman' by Whitney Houston. The adults are amazed at the ease in which Willa is singing this song. After all, not everyone can emulate Whitney, let alone a 5-year-old child. The adults brace themselves for the part where Willa has to modulate. If Willa can pull this off, she will be the talk of the town for days. With ease Willa reaches the high note, sending the crowd into a cheer of jubilation.

Everyone is dancing and having a good time. Joseph and Willow are dancing as well.

As Willa finishes her selection, Joseph brings the cake to her. It's an inside-out strawberry ice cream cake. This is Willa's absolute favorite cake in the whole gigantic world. Two years ago, Willow introduced her daughter to this cake when she baked it for New Year's Day. Willa has been obsessed with this type of cake ever since.

"All right Willa, make a wish and blow out the candles." Says Joseph.

Willa closes her eyes, makes a wish, and makes a blow at the candles. The candles don't go out. She makes a second attempt at blowing out the candles, but still no luck. She tries for a third, fourth, and fifth time, but with no success. It wasn't until she started to display some frustration that her daddy stepped in. Unable to keep a straight face, Joseph says while laughing,

"These are trick candles, Willa. They cannot be blown out."

"Daddy, you're always trying to trick me," she says while playfully hitting him.

That's Joseph when it came to his daughter. He is always playing pranks on her.

Joseph removes the trick candles and places real candles inside the cake. Five lit candles are now on the cake.

"All right Willa, make a wish and blow out these candles," daddy says with a smile on his face."

Willa closes her eyes, makes her wish, takes a deep breath, and blows out the candles with a heavy blow. Everyone is cheering and clapping for Willa. The crowd begins to sing the happy birthday song – The Stevie Wonder version.

"Okay Willa, it's time to cut the cake." Her mother says.

But Willa is not responding to her mother. She's just standing there in a daze for about 6 seconds.

"Oh, you're trying to get us back, Willa," says Joseph. Thinking she was getting him back for the trick-candles prank.

Willa then starts to act lethargic. She has her right hand to her head, and her left hand is wailing as if it was reaching for something. Two seconds later, Willa falls to the ground. Her body is twitching involuntarily, and she is foaming at the mouth. Panic fills the room as the grown-ups realize that Willa is having a seizure. Joseph goes to the ground to tend to his daughter. He holds her head and body in a loose yet firm grip, assuring that she does not get out of control. Joseph starts praying. He asks God to end this moment of distress. Willa continues to move irrepressibly. She scratches her face repeatedly. Everyone is freaking out. The children are frightened. They have never seen a person, let alone a child experience what Willa is currently experiencing. Willow doesn't know what to do. She too is in a frenzy.

"Joseph, do something," she yells.

"Willow, I'm trying. Someone call 9-1-1."

"I'm already on it, answers Mr. Gimber. An ambulance is on the way."

Willa's seizure slowly fades away, and Joseph is still holding her in his arms while on the floor. He softly caresses her head as they wait for the EMT to arrive. The ambulance arrives and immediately takes Willa to the nearest hospital.

Upon arriving at the hospital, blood tests are taken, and an MRI on Willa's brain is done. Two hours pass by with Joseph, Willow, and Willa all eagerly awaiting the tests results. The attending Doctor in the E.R., Dr. Zubinsky, approaches the Johnsons'

"Mr. and Mrs. Johnson, I'm afraid that your child probably has epilepsy. She has a scar on her brain the size of a penny. This scar will occasionally trigger the seizure attack she had today. The good news, however, is that her epilepsy can be managed with medication and good dieting."

31

"How in the world did she develop a scar on her brain?" Willow asks with a confused look.

"There's no way to know for sure," the doctor responds. "She could have been born with the scar, she could have hit her head one day while playing, or the scar could have simply developed on its own. The most important thing to do right now is to medicate her so that we can reduce the likelihood of this happening again."

"Okay doctor, but what about side-effects? I've heard stories about people feeling like zombies or being depressed," Joseph asks.

"Yes, there are side-effects in seizure prevention drugs, such as depression, fatigue, and suicidal thoughts. It is important that you monitor Willa and see if she is experiencing any of these effects. If she is, we can change the prescription. Each person responds differently to medication, so we won't know how she feels until after it's in her system. So I've done all I can do with her for now. I'm going to prepare the discharge papers. Please be sure to follow-up with Willa's pediatrician, and I'm going to give you a referral to a neurologist."

As Willow and Joseph prepare to take Willa home, Joseph immediately calls one of his deacons.

"Deacon Brown, contact as many members as you possibly can. We're going on a seven day fast."

When the Johnsons' arrive home, Joseph immediately goes to prayer. Willow is somewhat reticent this time. She usually would join Joseph in his prayer sessions. Willow is in shock from today's events. Willa noticed how reserved her mother appears.

"It's going to be okay, mommy. Don't you hear daddy praying? God will take care of me."

"You have your father's spirit, says Willow. You've inherited his level of faith."

"Don't you have faith too, mommy?"

"Well yes, I do. It's just…. Never mind. Let me give you a bath and get you ready for bed."

After putting Willa to bed, Joseph is still praying to God. Joseph was a praying man, but he has never prayed as hard or with so much anxiety as he is praying today. He's crying and begging God to remove this condition from his only child. When he ends his prayer, Willow comes into the bedroom to be with Joseph.

"Willow, how come you didn't join me in prayer? You know you're my prayer warrior, my backbone. I needed your energy today."

"I'm sorry Joseph. I guess I was just taken aback by seeing my baby go through all of this today. I can't imagine losing my daughter. I can't imagine how you would feel if she died."

"Hey don't talk that way, Willow. Our little girl ain't going nowhere."

"She's an amazing girl, Joseph. She is destined to be something special in this world. I just lost a little bit of faith today. I'm sorry."

"Sorry, sorry for what? You didn't do anything."

Willow begins to kiss her husband passionately. She wants him to make her feel good. She wants a moment where there is no pain.

Joseph kisses her back, and the two of them begin to take off each other's clothes. They make love passionately well into the night. After feeling neglected by his wife during his prayer session, Joseph once again feels whole, as he and his wife connect intimately.

Twenty-seven minutes later, and the Johnsons' have finished their lovemaking. They are still in bed but now yet asleep. Willow has her head pressed on Joseph's chest. Joseph has his arms wrapped around her. Willow wants to talk.

"Joseph?"

"Yes, my love."

"There's something I've wanted to ask you for years, but I've never had the guts to bring it up."

"Well ask away. I have nothing to hide from you."

"About eight years ago or so, on a Sunday evening during testimony service back at my dad's church, you asked the entire church to no longer call you JJ. You never told the church why. All you said was that God has transitioned you to a new dimension in your life and that you didn't want the name JJ to a part of that dimension. What's wrong with the name JJ? I miss calling you by that name."

"Usually when a person changes their name, it's because they are turning over a new leaf in their life."

"Yeah, or maybe the person is bipolar or has a split personality." She jokes.

"Well, that isn't the case with me, Willow. The name JJ is part of a chapter in my life that I'd rather not speak of, but I can already tell

34

that you're probably not going to let this go. So I'll tell you. Can you get up, please? I need you to sit up for this."

"Wow, is it that serious?" Willow asks.

"To me it is. Now I don't know if you know this or not, but I wasn't a virgin when we got married. Do you remember a young girl by the name of Gina, who used to attend your father's church?"

"Yeah, I remember her. Didn't she commit suicide back in Guyana?"

"Yes, that's right. And I'm the reason she committed suicide. You see, one Sunday morning, we had sex in the minister's study room. The spirit of God revealed this to Gina's mother, and Gina was sent home to Guyana. So if it weren't for JJ, Gina might still be here in America."

"Okay Joseph, I hear what you're saying. But I have a confession. I was there when you and Gina were having sex."

"You were what! What do you mean you were there?"

"Well, you see, my dad sent me downstairs to the study room to get his robe for him. While I was searching for the robe, I heard you and Gina coming in. I was wondering what ya'll were up to, so I hid in the closet. I kept the door cracked so that I could watch you two. Call me crazy, but I was kind of turned on by the fact that you two would be so bold as to have sex in the basement of the church. Anyway, I noticed that something startled you two and you both ran back upstairs. Since I was a teenager, I've been attracted to you, but watching you do your thing that day increased my fascination for you. I wanted you to be my man, but I wasn't going to throw myself at you either. All the same, that's no reason not to want to be known as JJ."

"Well, there's more, Willow. About a week before I hooked up with Gina, I had a threesome with two women. That was when I lost my virginity."

"So you lost your virginity during a threesome? Weren't you a little freak back in the day! Still, that's no reason to change your name."

"But I'm not done, Willow."

"There's more, Joseph?"

"Yes, after the threesome and hooking up with Gina, I then slept with a married woman. Her name is Karen. She was my childhood crush. It wasn't just the fornication that was wrong; it was also my temper. I once threatened to beat up my boss. It was as if Satan had a hold on me. Anyway, one day, the voice of God spoke to me during a time when I was witnessing. He showed me all the angels that were fighting against demons. It was a sight that I don't think I'd ever want to see again. You're not going to believe what I'm about to say, but God used me to defend the demons from beating the angels. From that day forward, God elevated me to a higher level of apostolic ministry. So part of my metamorphosis is to be no longer called JJ. JJ is a boy who got caught up in sin and almost didn't make it out. Had it not been for the grace of God, I would be deeper into sin and not the man you see before you tonight. So this is why I ask that no one refers to me as JJ. Not now, not ten years from now, and not even at my funeral."

Willow sat there observing the raw emotion coming from Joseph. She can see that he was dead serious about his name. She thought JJ was a cute nickname for her hubby. But as a pastor, JJ didn't want to be looked at as being cute, but instead, a solemn man of God.

"Okay honey, I get it. I won't call you JJ, nor will I let anyone else call you JJ. No matter what, I will always love you. So can I ask you another question?

"Sure, what is it?"

"How was the threesome?"

"Good night, Willow." He says smiling back at his wife. "Go to bed," as he ignores her question.

Willow smiles, kisses her man good night, and goes to sleep.

Meanwhile, back in the Mauna Loa volcano, Krimion approaches Satan's throne. Satan is looking as handsome as ever. He is relishing in some of his latest conquests. In his possession are the souls of some influential people of earth. Satan sees Krimion approaching him.

"Krimion, what are you doing here?"

"My Lord, phase 1 of Joseph mission is complete."

"Phase 1, huh? And what exactly was phase 1?"

"I gave his daughter a seizure. Right on her birthday at that. They spent most of the day in the hospital. The girl has epilepsy. This won't be her last seizure. I'll make sure of that."

"Okay, so you gave his daughter a seizure. So what! Sansar could have done that."

"Yes, but as I said, this is phase 1. Plus something else fell right into my lap, but I won't get ahead of myself just yet. I will be putting phase 2 into motion shortly. Satan, I assure you, Joseph is going to be yours soon."

"You seem very confident in yourself, Krimion. Go on now and get back to Joseph. Oh, and Krimion?"

"Yes, my lord."

"Don't you ever go to heaven without my permission! Only God could have allowed you to inflict disease on the little girl in such a short span of time. It takes days or months for a demon to inflict a human with sickness. The only way you could have done this is if you went to Jehovah for permission. Only I can go before Jehovah with a request unless I designate someone to go in my stead. Do this again, and next time I will feed you to the hounds like I'm about to do to this poor soul."

Satan then takes the soul of Wesley Hamilton and feeds him to the hounds. Wesley was a former gospel singer who crossed over into pop music. He got heavily involved in drugs and died of an overdose. Wesley can be heard screaming in pain and begging for help.

"Jesus, Jesus help me!"

"Sorry, Wesley, Jesus doesn't live here. Here is a place for sinners. You can't call him here."

38

Satan then begins to remix the words to a famous American Christian chorus.

'Jesus ain't on the Hell line; you can't tell him what you want.'

'Oh, Jesus ain't on the Hell line; you can't tell him what you want.'

'Jesus ain't on the Hell line; you can't tell him what you want.'

'You can't call him up and tell him what you want.'

Krimion watches in admiration as Satan taunts his latest victim. Krimion loves the way Satan exhibits his wickedness. Krimion looks up to Satan, the way Satan looked up to God.

"My lord, soon you'll be able to do similar things to Joseph. I just wanted you to know that I'll be needing about twenty soldiers for phase two and three of my plans."

"Do as you wish, Krimion. I am granting you unlimited resources for this mission. Therefore, you have no excuse to fail."

"And fail I shall not, my king." What Joseph is about to go through will be worse than what you put Job through, thousands of years ago. But unlike Job, Joseph will indeed, curse God and die."

"Krimion, if I didn't know better, I'd swear you just insulted me. Don't make me get angry with you, boy."

"Oh no, my King, I'm simply drawing a comparison. No slight intended."

"Good! Now get out of my face and go back to Pastor Johnson. And this time, don't come back to me unless Joseph is here with you!"

"As you wish, my Lord."

Krimion marches off from Satan, informs several other devils of what their upcoming roles will be, and heads back to Brooklyn.

It is now Sunday morning, and Krimion arrives at Joseph's church, twenty minutes into the service. By this time, all the members are aware of Willa's medical condition. Krimion can hear the members praising God in song and dance. They know that if they reach out to God outwardly, God will heal Willa from her epilepsy. Willa is there singing and praising God with the members. For a five-year-old girl, she is not shy at all. Her eyes are closed, her hands are lifted up in complete surrender and benevolence to her God.

Five minutes later and the worship is over. Joseph approaches the podium to deliver his sermon. As usual, Joseph provides a timely, and inspiring message. He calls for his daughter to come to the front of the church. He signals for the deacons to stand by his side. Joseph rests his right hand on the forehead of Willa and begins praying for her. He commands the sickness that is upon her to be cast away. The entire congregation is in one accord as they too beseech their God on Willa's behalf. About thirty seconds into the prayer, Willa's body begins to shake.

"Help me, Jesus," she cries out loud.

"Help her, Lord," echoes some of the members.

Joseph closes the prayer, pronouncing complete healing and deliverance for Willa.

"Now little girl, walk off in faith, believing that you are healed," he orders his daughter.

Willa does as commanded and the congregation praises God in agreement for her healing.

Krimion now takes this opportunity to disrupt the positivity of the service. He walks by the side of Willa, touches the right side of her head, and causes Willa to have another seizure. This time, her body collapses to her right. As she is falling, her head hits the side of one of the wooden pews. While on the floor, Krimion has his hands pressed down on her chest to keep her from moving and to prevent anyone from picking her up. Just like the first time, she is foaming at the mouth and also scratching her face.

Willow is freaking out. "No, not again!" she screams. Joseph runs over to assist his daughter. He attempts to cast away this evil spell that is upon his only child.

"In the name of Jesus Christ, I command this seizure to cease, right away! I command any evil spirit that is tormenting my child to go back from whence you came."

Krimion is laughing at Joseph and the entire congregation. He knows that cannot halt his demonizing of Willa. Mother Berry, a sixty-five-year-old member, can sense Krimion. She starts speaking in an unknown language that no one in the church can understand. Over and over, she is saying one particular phrase. "Krepta anga deblaco es Grilla, Krimion. Krepta ango deblaco es Grilla, Krimion. This is interpreted, "Get away from the girl, Krimion. Get away from the girl, Krimion!" Only Krimion understood what she was saying. Krimion can sense the power of God upon the woman and leaves the scene.

41

But the damage to Willa had already been done. Her seizure has ended, but she is barely conscious. Calls to 9-1-1 were already made. Willow and Joseph sit next to Willa crying and asking God why this is happening to their only child.

Upon arriving at the hospital, more x-rays and cat-scans are done. The scar in Willa's brain has enlarged. The doctors had never seen a minor scar grow in size within such a short span of time. The team of doctors recommends to the Johnsons that they increase the dosage of Lamotrigine prescribed to Willa. Reluctantly, they agree. Concern about the side-effects with such a high dosage is on the mind of Willow. But seeing the state her daughter was in, she knew this was the best thing for her child.

The doctors agree to admit Willa to the hospital for two weeks of observation. Willow decided that she was not going to leave her daughter's side until she was discharged. Joseph did not object to Willow's decision. He wishes that he could do the same, but he still had a church to run, a mortgage, and soon to be medical bills to pay.

The next day, Joseph visits Willa early at six O'clock in the morning.

Willa is in pretty good spirits, considering what she had been through. She is laughing, playing games on her tablet, conversing with her mom, and making friends with the other kid patients on her floor of the hospital. She is recovering pretty well, but due to her age, the doctors want to wait the full two weeks before discharging the young child.

Two weeks pass and the doctors feel comfortable with Willa's progress and decide to discharge her tomorrow morning.

Joseph is home preparing the house for Willa's return. Joseph has never prayed as hard as he did while Willa was in the hospital. He barely ate and had lost ten pounds. But once he heard of his little angel's release, his demeanor changed, and he was back to his usual happy go lucky self.

It is now 5 p.m. when Joseph's doorbell rings.

"Just a second. I'll be right there."

He runs to the door, looks through the door window, and is in complete shock as to who he sees on the other side of the door. A young lady with a little boy standing next to her. Joseph recognizes the lady and opens the door.

"Karen?"

"Hi JJ! It's been a long time."

"Yes, it has, Karen. Almost seven years or so."

"More like eights years, eight months, and 24 days."

"Wow, okay Karen. You were always good at keeping up with dates. Would you like to come in?"

"Are you sure that's okay? I don't want to offend Mrs. Johnson."

"Yes, it's okay. Mrs. Johnson isn't here, but even if she were here, she wouldn't mind."

"Oh, okay," she replies as she enters his house.

43

"And who's this young man, Karen? Is this your son?"

"Yes, it is, JJ. This is my son, Favor."

"Favor? His name is Favor?" He asks.

"Yes, JJ. His name is Favor."

"Well, I think that is quite a unique name that you have given him. I can see God's favor all over the young boy."

Joseph looks at the little boy and smiles at him.

"Karen, you got yourself one handsome looking boy here. Wait til he gets older. The girls are going to be all over him."

"Yeah, he is quite charming. I guess he takes after his dad."

"So what brings you here to my place Karen? I mean we haven't spoken since the day after we last slept together. Neither one of us called or texted each other."

"Did you think about me, JJ? Did you ever wonder what I was up to?" She asks?

"Of course I did. But I started dating my wife, Willow. Then I started my church, and then, you know, life moved on."

"I know, JJ. And I know all about your marriage and your church. I've been secretly keeping tabs on you through friends and social media. I am so happy for all of your success. God has truly blessed you, JJ. The reason I came to see you today, is because my husband Gregory and I are getting a divorce. He kicked me out of the house yesterday. And I am ashamed to go to my parents' house."

44

"I'm so sorry to hear that, Karen. Oh by the way, before we continue this conversation, can you do me one favor?"

"Sure, what's that?"

"Can you not call me JJ? I prefer Joseph. JJ refers to a time in my life that I'd rather forget."

"Oh, you mean the time in your life when you and I had an affair?" Suggested Karen.

"Well, that's part of it, but it is more than just our affair. I made a lot of bad choices, so omitting the nickname JJ is like turning over a new leaf for me. It's nothing personal toward you. It's just my preference at this time."

"Okay J - I mean Joseph. I'll respect your wishes."

"Good! So tell me, what happened between you and your husband? Why would he kick you and your son out of the house?"

"All right, but can I send Favor somewhere so I can tell you in private?"

"That's fine with me. Favor can stay here in the living room, while you and I go to the dining room to talk."

"Favor, mommy is gonna go talk with Mr. Johnson for a sec. you stay here and watch TV or play with your tablet, okay?"

"Okay mommy," answers the little boy.

Joseph and Karen walk into the dining room. Karen takes a seat while Joseph pours her a glass of water.

"Okay, Karen, talk to me!"

"Well, it all started when family members were trying to figure out if Favor looked like Gregory or like me. It's funny because when a baby is just born, everyone starts talking about who the child resembles. But in reality, the child hasn't developed enough to get a good idea as to who he looks like. From the time of Favor's birth, all anyone would say is how much he looked like his father. But as Favor got older, the resemblance was not as obvious. And he wasn't taking after me either. Gregory started asking me if there was a chance that someone else could be the father. I vehemently denied any possibility of that. I swore to him that I was faithful to him through and through. Of course, that was a lie. This man was so sure he wasn't the father that he tried to get us to go on one of those talk shows where they do DNA testing for free. I vetoed that idea right away. I mean there's no way I was about to have me and my family embarrassed, no matter what the outcome was going to be."

While Karen is talking, Joseph opens the dining room doors and takes a peek at Favor. He was listening intensely to Karen while in profound observance of Favor. Right away he realizes what's going on, but wants to hear it from Karen's mouth.

"So after several years of denying my unfaithfulness to him or any chance of him not being the father, I finally confessed about our affair. Needless to say, he was livid. I mean I've never seen him get as angry toward me like this before. Not that I could blame him; I was unfaithful to him. This man not only worshipped the ground I walked on, but he worshipped the very air that I breathed. To say that he was hurt is an understatement. Anyway, he immediately asked for a paternity test. We went to court to get this done. The DNA results confirmed what he believed; he is not the father of Favor."

"We were still living together the day of the results. We even made love a few days before. After the results, he asked me who the potential father could be."

Joseph looked at Karen with fear, anticipating what she was about to say.

"No, no, no, Karen! You didn't mention my name now, did you? Joseph was afraid of Gregory. He was a former club bouncer. Joseph never met the man, but he has seen pictures of Gregory during his high school wrestling days."

"Yes, Joseph. I told him of our affair. And I told him what I now want to tell you. Favor is your son."

"Joseph is not shocked by what he has just heard. He is, however, a bit annoyed that he is finding this out now."

"No, no, no," he says. "Why now, Lord! Why now?"

"Excuse me!" Responds Karen. "I mean, I didn't expect you to be all jumping up for joy, but I need you to be ready to take care of your son."

"Karen, you don't understand. I'm going through so much right now. My daughter, Willa, is in the hospital. She's had two seizures recently. She's been in the hospital for the past few weeks and will be coming home tomorrow. Karen, what am I supposed to tell my wife? She's going to freak out. And my church! Do you know how many members I could lose over this? People can be very judgmental you know. And why didn't you come to me a long time ago when you first found out you were pregnant? You knew there would be a chance that I was the father."

47

"JJ, I mean Joseph, I didn't want to risk losing my husband. He has been the best husband any woman can ask for. Plus, I knew that you had moved on with your life. I didn't want to mess up what plans God had intended for you. Trust me, Joseph, if I could have continued to keep the real identity of Favor's father from being revealed, I would have. But the truth came out and I have to handle it, and I hope you can too."

"So what do you expect me to do with you and Favor now, Karen? It's not like I can move you into my house."

"Well, Gregory kicked me out with nothing to live off of. He was the bread-winner of the home, while I was a stay at home mom. I have no money, no stocks, nothing liquid. Maybe you can loan me some hotel money until I get myself situated."

"Yeah, I can do that. Let's go to the bank and I'll withdraw some cash for you. I'll give you two thousand dollars. That should help you survive for now. Please don't go to some expensive hotel. You need to make this money last a little while."

"Thank you, Joseph. I really appreciate your help."

"You're welcome, Karen. Now I have to figure out what I am going to say to my wife. She's going to be devastated to learn that I have a male child. We've been trying to get pregnant again. She wants to give me a son, an heir to follow after me as pastor of the church. I don't know what to do, but I'll figure something out. Anyway, let's go to the bank and then I'll take you to a motel to stay".

"No, Joseph, you're taking me a hotel, not a motel. I am not staying in some seman-stained, bedbug-infested motel. I'm not asking to go to some five-star hotel, but I need something decent and comfortable for your son."

"All right Karen. Fine, I know just the place where you can go. Now let's get out of here before my wife gets home".

In the background to the far right of the dining room, stood Krimion. Smirking with joy over the additional ammunition he now has to add to his arsenal of weapons in his quest for Joseph's soul. As Joseph leaves with Karen and Favor for the bank, Krimion stays around to snoop through the house for things he can use to his advantage. He goes through their file cabinets and looks over their tax returns. Next, he searches through all the drawers in the living and dining rooms. He heads into the master bedroom and examines the drawers of Joseph and Willow. He searches thoroughly through Willow's drawers, not finding anything of value. He then goes through her giant box of maxi-pad supplies and finds an unexpected item in there.

"Jackpot!" He yells, with wicked glee. "I'll just leave this pretty little item out in the open for Joseph to see. I'm sure he'll have some questions for Willow after he sees this."

Krimion exits the Johnson home. Everything is falling right into place for him.

Meanwhile, Joseph has already gone to the bank to withdraw some cash and has taken Karen and Favor to a hotel to stay in for a week.

After he drops them off, he calls his wife to check up on her and Willa.

"Hey baby, how are you and Willa doing?"

49

"We're fine. Willa has been asleep all day pretty much. I've been by her side, making sure another seizure doesn't come upon her."

"Okay, well I'm coming to pick you up. I figured we could have some husband and wife time together. Plus, I need to talk to you about something."

"Oh no, Joseph. Don't come to the hospital. I'm heading out. Gonna go to the gym and work off this stress."

"How bout you work off your stress with me, tonight, in the bedroom?"

"Yes, Joseph, she says with a smile. We can do that too. But I have to go to the gym first. I've put on some weight since Willa was admitted."

"And I've lost some weight during the same time. I guess we're handling our stress differently. Well, I'm going to head back home then, and wait for you there. See you soon, love".

"See you, Joseph."

Joseph starts to head home, but 5 minutes into his drive, he decides to head to the hospital to see his little girl. He didn't care if she was asleep or not. He just wanted to see her beautiful little face.

Upon arriving at the hospital and approaching the room door for Willa, Joseph comes across Nurse Harrington. She has been assigned to the care of Willa ever since her first day of admission.

"Good evening," Nurse!

"Good evening, Mr. Johnson. I see someone's excited that their little girl is going home tomorrow."

"You got that right, Nurse. God is good. The devil is putting my family through a trying time, but I know my God gave us the power and authority to overcome all obstacles. I thank God for the staff here at the hospital. They've done an amazing job with my daughter. And although she hasn't received the immediate healing I was hoping for, I know that through the doctor's instruction, Willa will be just fine."

"That's right Mr. Johnson. God is in control, but he has placed knowledgeable doctors to give your girl the best treatment possible. And with his help, we were able to give Willa the proper care needed. Well, I'll let you go now. I am sure she would love the company today. She was wondering when you or Mrs. Johnson would come to see her."

"What are you talking about, Nurse? My wife was here not too long ago."

"I don't recall seeing her today, sir. But perhaps she came while I was on the other side of the floor, dealing with other patients."

"Yeah, I'm sure that's what it is. Willow has been here non-stop over the duration of Willa's stay."

"Alright then, I'm sure I'm mistaken. Well go in and see your daughter before visiting hours come to an end."

Joseph walks into Willa's room and sees his daughter sitting up-right in her bed, watching cartoons on TV.

"Daddy! I missed you."

"I missed you too, princess. Did the doctors tell you that you're are going home tomorrow?"

"Yes they did, daddy. And I can't wait to be in my own bed again. I miss our house. I miss playing in our backyard. I hope things will go back to normal."

"Things will go back to normal, Willa. But it's going to take time. Your epilepsy has to be monitored daily. Mommy and I have to be very careful with you from now on."

"Daddy, can't you just pray to God and command my disease to go away like you've done for other people?"

"Yes Willa, I've been praying to God for you. For some reason, he is not ready to heal you. Sometimes in life, we don't always get what we want when we want it. Sometimes we have to wait days, months, or even years."

"I don't wanna wait that long daddy. You told me to believe in God. You told me that he is a healer. You told me that a long time ago you healed a man from a heart attack after praying to God. So why hasn't God healed me after you prayed to him?"

"I don't know Willa. But we must never lose faith in God. Sometimes God allows us to go through a time of sickness or a time of bad luck so that we can pray to him more, so that a greater purpose would be revealed. All I know is that sooner or later, God is going to show you that he has your back. So I can understand why you might not believe in God's healing power as strongly as I do, but I am asking you to promise me that you will trust me and not lose faith in Him. Okay, princess?"

"Okay, daddy. I know that you know best. I love you, daddy."

"I love you too, princess. Now get some rest. Tomorrow you're busting out of this joint. I have to go home and get the place ready for your return. Plus, I need to talk to your mother about some things."

Joseph gives Willa a hug and a kiss on the cheek.

"See you later daddy. Tell mommy that I missed her today."

"Okay, princess. I will."

Joseph heads back to his car and proceeds to drive home. While in the car, he starts to wonder why his wife lied to him about being at the hospital today. He begins to wonder about all types of things. Was she with another man? Had she been lying about being at the hospital on other days also? Had she been too stressed out to visit Willa today? And if so, why couldn't she have just said this to him. Joseph and Willow have always had an open and honest relationship with each other. Now Joseph sees that Willow is keeping something from him. Also, he still has to tell her about Karen and his son, Favor. Joseph starts getting a headache from just thinking about all of this and decides to leave Willow's dishonesty alone for a few days and tell her about his son at another time.

Three weeks later

It is Saturday morning at the Resnick residence. Alex and his wife are ready to head out to the synagogue for their Sabbath service. Although Alex was a busy businessman, he rarely neglected his duties to his place of worship. The temple is only five blocks away, so he and his wife decide to walk their way there.

As they stroll down the street, Mr. Resnick is holding his wife's hand. It is a beautiful sunny day, with a bit of a breeze coming from the west. Mr. Resnick has a slight cold that has been plaguing him for the past three days. Walking toward them are five young black men, who look to be anywhere from the ages of eighteen to mid-twenties. The young men are wearing dark colored jeans. They each have on either black or brown hoodies, with the hoods over their heads. Mrs. Resnick is a bit paranoid of the young men and makes a suggestion to her husband:

"Let's cross the street right now, Alex. I don't trust those guys approaching us."

"Nonsense, Rita. They are just black men coming from the store or going to the mall. Let's not judge them based on their outward appearance. I've met some fine young men in jeans and hoodies."

The five men draw closer to the Resnicks' They are within seven feet of each other. Alex's cold starts to act up again. He is coughing and sneezing profusely. The wind is picking up as well. The five men walk past the Resnicks'. Three walk to the left of Alex and two step to the right of Rita. Alex has a thick chunk of phlegm to spit out. He turns his face to the right and spits the phlegm out of his mouth. At the

54

same time, the wind picks up some more and carries the spit behind Alex and onto one of the young black men.

James looks at the back of his left hand and sees the most disgusting, the most sickening, and the most repulsive chunk of spit on his left index and pinky fingers.

He turns around to Alex and his wife.

"Yo. Did you just spit on me, man?"

"Oh no, I'm sorry about that. Did it land on you? I have a…"

"Did it land on me? Did it land on me? You ask. Yes, you dummy it landed on me. What, you think you're better than me? Yo Taj, this guy thinks he can spit on me because he's better than me," James says to one of his other friends.

"No, it was an accident," interrupts Rita. "My husband has a bad cold."

"Man, that's bull!" Says another one of the hooded men, named Martin. "Your husband had plenty of room in front of him to spit."

"We saw ya'll looking at us and talking about us from a distance. Ya'll have a problem with black people in this neighborhood?"

Rita starts speaking to Alex in her Yiddish tongue. She is saying, 'See, I told you we should have crossed the street earlier.'

"Yo, speak English in front of me!" Yells James.

James walks up to Alex, takes the back of his hand wipes it on Alex's blazer. And then without notice, he kicks Alex in the scrotum, punches him in his face and walks off with his friends.

55

Rita is frantic.

"Oh my God, Oh my God. Alex, are you alright. Why did you do this?" She screams to James while he's walking away. "I'm calling the police."

"No, don't call the police. I'm okay. Just give me a minute, and I'll be fine."

"What do you mean don't call the police? That hoodlum just assaulted you!"

"It's alright, Rita. The whole thing was just a misunderstanding. Let me get up and we can be on our way."

Alex stands to his feet, adjusts his clothes, grabs his wife by the hand, and walks to the temple.

As he reaches the temple, he is greeted at the front door by Rabbi Shapiro.

"Alex, so good to see you. Hey, what happened to your lips? Why are you bleeding?"

"He was beaten up by a street thug." Says his wife.

"It's okay, Rabbi. He thought that I intentionally spat on him. He overreacted, but I don't wanna make a big deal about it."

"Tell me Alex, was this guy black?"

"Yes, he was," chimed Rita. "There were five of them there. All in dark-colored hoodies."

"This neighborhood has been in a downward spiral ever since the blacks came into this neighborhood," says, the Rabbi. "The sidewalks are dirty and the property value of homes has since declined. They play their music as loud as ever, well past midnight. Now they want to assault one of us? I will not stand for this. We must strike back."

"Strike back? Are you kidding me?" Asks Alex. "You want to start a race war with African Americans. Have you been paying attention to what's been going on throughout the country over the past ten years? Striking back is not necessary. Besides, we are God's children; war is always the last resort. Now let's go inside, put this behind us, and pray for those young men."

"Alright, Alex," replies the Rabbi. "You were never one for confrontation."

So the Resnicks' and the Rabbi all go in for their Sabbath service.

As service ends, Alex makes a quick call to Joseph. He wants to check up on Willa, but he also wanted to answer some questions Joseph had about property taxes on the church.

Joseph doesn't answer the call, but texts Alex back two minutes later, requesting that Alex meet him by the church in an hour. Alex agrees to do so. When Alex reaches the church, he sees a few of the men doing some minor repairs to the building. Joseph walks over to Alex, and they begin to discuss property taxes and other expenses the building has. While they are talking Alex can't help but have his eyes fastened to one of the gentlemen painting the side of the building. After two minutes of talking, Joseph notices that he doesn't have Alex's undivided attention.

"Alex, what's wrong? Why are you looking so hard at one of my men?"

57

"That young man over there assaulted me earlier today."

"What? Are you sure?"

"Yes, I'm sure. We walked past each other on my way to temple and I accidentally spat on him. He was with some other friends. He thought that I spat on him on purpose, so he beat me up. I didn't call the police when he left, but seeing him over there is making me uneasy."

"Well, I'm going to fix this mess right now. Hey James, James. Come over here."

James walks over and to Joseph and recognizes Alex.

"Yes sir, pastor Johnson."

"Did you assault this man here, earlier today?"

James was quiet, not wanting to answer.

"C'mon now son, answer the question. Did you assault this man right here?"

"Yes! Yes, I did, James barked. And I'd do it again. These Jews around here are so smug. They walk around like they're God's gift to the world. They own all of the property and rent out their apartments to us poor black people at enormous prices. They control a majority of the currency across the world and are abusers of the welfare system more than any other race of people in America. Then this guy over here had the nerve to spit on me today. Hell no! I wasn't taking that mess from him today. Not today and not ever. My mother's landlord is a Jew and he's a real jerk. He cuts off the hot water if my mom is one day late with the rent. One day late and you have no grace?

Joseph proceeds to interject his thoughts.

"So James, it seems to me that you have an issue with Jews in general."

"Yes I do, pastor. I can't stand them."

"Well, let me tell you about this gentleman here whom you assaulted. His name is Alex Resnick. Alex and his cousin sold me this building here, the very same building you are painting. It was sold to me at a discounted price. Mr. Resnick has been nothing but gracious toward my members and me. If not for him, we'd still be in a store-front building. So as far as I'm concerned, he's family. He is my brother and you have offended my brother. With that being said, you are also my brother. And it hurts me to see two of my brothers at odds with each other."

"Well, this Jew ain't my brother, pastor. He could drop dead for all I care. He means nothing to me."

"Now James I think you need to go inside the church, get a drink of water, and take a moment to calm down."

"Man, I don't need to calm down. But I do need to get the hell out of here before I punch this guy in the face. Heil Hitler, Mr. Resnick. Heil Hitler."

Joseph is shocked and enraged by what he just heard come out of the lips of James. Now James is bigger and stronger than Joseph, but Joseph was so furious by what he just heard James say that he grabs James by the collar of his shirt.

"Are you out of your mind, boy? Do you know what you have just said and how offensive that language truly is? I don't think you truly

59

do. What you have just said is the equivalent to a white man calling you nigger. Now you apologize to Mr. Resnick right now for your offensive language to him."

"Man, I'm outta here!" Pouts James as he runs away from the church.

"I'm sorry about James' behavior." Apologizes Joseph to Alex. James is a young man whom I am trying to guide in the right path. His father has been in prison since James was four years old. His mother died of a drug overdose when he was twelve. He hasn't a positive role model in his life. Still, this is no excuse for the way he treated you. Hopefully, he will calm down and see the error of his ways."

"Joseph, your apology is unnecessary. But I thank you anyway. I'm gonna be frank with you; my Rabbi wasn't happy when he saw my bruised up face today. When I told him what happened, he wanted to try and get even. I had to talk him out of that, but if this type of thing happens again, with me or any of my other fellow Jews, this could turn into Crown Heights again."

"Alex, are you referring to the infamous clash between Jews and African Americans back in the 1990s?"

"That's right. I know you weren't born when that happened, but I suppose you heard and read about the incident, or shall I say incidents. Lives were lost, people were severely hurt. The Crown Heights community was split. Jews vs. Blacks. It wasn't pretty at all, Joseph. I know for a fact that God wasn't pleased at all during that time. I would hate to see another Crown Heights in this area, today."

"Well, hopefully, cooler heads will prevail and the Spirit of God will be an influence in all of us."

"I pray you're right, Joseph. Well, let me get back to my wife before she files a missing person's report with the police. I think she's just one more incident from a panic attack."

"Okay, Alex. You do that," Joseph laughed. "I'll give you a call if I have any more property tax questions."

Alex went home to his wife and informed her of his second encounter with James at the church. Rita was fuming when she heard how James disrespected Alex as well as Jews in general.

"How dare that boy speak to you in such language! He has no respect for elders or the history of our people. That boy needs to be taught manners."

"That's the thing, Rita. He has no parents. His father is in prison and his mother died when he was twelve. I know it's hard but I need you to cut him some slack."

Rita walks away frustrated and starts venting in her Yiddish tongue. This is not over, as far as she is concerned.

The clock hits 5:30 AM. It's Sunday morning, and Joseph wakes up to get ready for church. Willow is already up cooking breakfast. Joseph didn't get much sleep, as his mind had been racing with thoughts of the James and Alex incident, to his Karen dilemma, to Willow lying to him about being at the hospital with Willa. Plus, Joseph had another issue to confront Willow about. He texts his assistant pastor and tells him to prepare to preach the afternoon sermon for today.

Willa would not be up for another two hours, so Joseph decides that now would be the best time to confront Willow. He walks downstairs and heads to the kitchen. Even with a head-tie and nightgown on, Willow still looks like a sexy Nubian Queen. Joseph is almost tempted to lure his wife into a quick moment of sexual pleasure. But he quickly snaps out of his moment of lust and walks into the kitchen.

"Good morning, babe. Would you like some tea while you wait for your breakfast?" Willow asks.

"No thanks, love. Actually, I need you to stop cooking and sit down. I have a few important things that I need to speak to you about."

"But I'm in the middle of cooking. Can it wait like 10 minutes?"

"No, not really. What we need to talk about has been on my mind all night. I am sleep deprived because of this."

"Okay, then what is it?" She nervously asks.

"So there are so many things I need to say to you, but I will start with this. First and foremost, understand that I love you with all my heart."

"I love you too, Joseph."

"Secondly, understand that I have never, ever been unfaithful to you."

"Okay." Responds Willow, a little concerned now.

"But a few weeks ago, I found out that I have a 7-year-old son."

"A what?" She screams. "You're kidding me, right? Is this some sort of a joke? Okay, Okay, you got me. Where's the camera? You're always messing with me, Joseph. Ha, ha, ha!"

"This is no joke, Willow. Remember I told you that eight years ago I slept with my childhood crush, Karen?"

"Yes, I remember."

"Well a couple of weeks ago, she unexpectedly came here to the house. She had a little boy with her. She said that her husband kicked her out after a DNA test proved he wasn't the father. She said that I am the father. I gave her $2,000 to stay in a hotel until she gets herself settled. I'm going to order a DNA test for myself, to remove any doubt. But let me tell ya, Willow. That little boy looks just like me. It was frightening how the resemblance was so striking."

"Willow's mind starts to race will all sorts of thoughts. Part of her wants to curse her husband out, while another part of her wants to accuse Karen of trying to sabotage her marriage. She wants to play cool, but she also wants to show her disappointment.

"Joseph, this is ridiculous. You have a son with another woman. A son, Joseph. I don't believe this. Are you sure you're the father? How do you know that she's not just trying to squeeze her way back into your life now that you're a pastor of a mega-church?

63

"You're right, Willow. I don't know anything for sure right now. But what I do know is that if the boy is my son, I'm going to be a responsible man and take care of him."

"This is crazy, Joseph. So you mean you weren't smart enough to put on a condom back then?"

"Well on one occasion, we didn't use protection."

"Oh, so ya'll had sex multiple times? Let me ask you this, do you love her?"

"Love her? No way. My heart belongs to you. I'd forgotten all about her until she came to the house, that is. She came to the house the day before Willa was released from the hospital. I was going to tell you then, but some other issues came up and I decided to leave it alone."

"Wait a minute. What other issues could have come up that would have prevented you from revealing me of this bombshell?"

"Well, before I get into that, I kinda want to conclude the current topic regarding my son."

Willow is pacing back and forth. Thoughts are racing, anxiety is kicking in. She wonders to herself: What else does he have to confess? Is he going to leave me for Karen and his new son? How will this news affect his pastoralship?

"Willow, I just want to reiterate that if the boy is mine, I will be the best father to him that I can be."

"I guess you have your son now." She responds.

"I'll address that in a few minutes." He answers. "I want to talk about something else now."

"Oh yeah, what's that?"

"This has more to do with you, Willow. The evening before Willa was discharged from the hospital, I called your phone, and you said you were at the hospital but were about to leave for the gym."

"Yeah, and?"

"Well, I went to the hospital to see Willa and the nurse told me that she didn't see you. Also, Willa mentioned that she missed you that day. So my question to you is, where were you that day and why did you lie to me?"

Unbeknownst to Willow and Joseph, but Krimion is in the kitchen with them, listening to their conversation. He whispers in the ears of Willow.

"Oh, so you're keeping tabs on me now, Joseph? Can't a woman have a day to herself without being questioned?"

"Willow, please don't deflect from my question. No one is keeping tabs on you. You are my wife, ya know! I have a right to know where you were. Imagine if that were me lying to you. You wouldn't stop until I gave you an answer. So please tell me, where were you?"

"Okay Joseph, I'll tell you."

Willow pours herself a cup of tea, adds one spoon of sugar, and starts talking while stirring her drink.

"Since Willa has been in the hospital, I've started smoking weed."

"Weed? Are you for real?"

"Yes, Joseph. I've been going to my Cousin Ben's house and been smoking there. The issue with Willa had me all stressed out. I needed something to relieve the stress and weed was the answer."

"Hey weed isn't the worst drug in the world to take, but weed isn't the answer. Jesus is the answer."

"I have faith in Jesus, Joseph. But my anxiety was at an all-time high. Praying didn't seem to help. I knew that if I had told you what I was doing, you would've freaked out."

"Maybe I would have freaked out momentarily, but I would have had some sort of understanding and would have tried to accept what you were doing. But okay, fine. At least now I know what you were doing that day."

"Okay good. Now can I finish preparing breakfast before our daughter wakes up?"

"No, not yet, my love. There's one more thing."

"Oh boy! What is it now?"

"So when I went back home that night from visiting Willa, I was cleaning up our room and couldn't help but notice the case of birth control pills in your tampon box. May I ask, how long have you been on birth control, and were you ever planning on telling me?"

"Joseph, why are you snooping around in my personal stuff? That's an invasion of privacy. You've gone too far now, Joseph. Too far!"

66

"I've gone too far, you say. I'm not the one hiding birth control pills from her husband. I thought you wanted to give me a son?"

"Well, it seems like you've gotten that taken care of with Karen."

"Oh stop it, Willow. I still want a son with you. That hasn't changed. But it has been five years, and you haven't gotten pregnant yet. Those pills seem to explain why."

"No, those pills explain that they are pills."

"Willow, you are beating around the bush. Are the pills yours or not? Stop stalling."

"I'm holding them for someone. One of my students at the school wanted to go on birth control, but her mother wouldn't allow her. She's sexually active with her boyfriend, so I agreed to get pills for her in my name. I store them here for her, obviously, so that her mother doesn't find it in their house."

"So Willow if that's all it is, why couldn't you have told this to me? Why be so secretive? What am I supposed to think if I find a bunch of birth control pills hidden inside a case of tampons?"

"I get it, Joseph. I messed up. I haven't been as forthcoming with you as I should have. I've been keeping some things from you that I shouldn't have and that's no way to keep a marriage happy and healthy. I'm sorry Joseph. Please forgive me."

"Of course I forgive you. You know you mean the world to me. I just don't want you keeping secrets from me. Now let's promise to never keep things from each other ever again."

"I promise, Joseph. It won't happen again."

So Joseph and Willow managed to work things out. Willow seems to be in acceptance that Joseph may be the father of a son from a marital affair. Joseph accepted Willow's explanation of the whereabouts the day he went to visit Willa in the hospital, as well as her explanation of why she had birth control pills in the house.

Willow finishes making breakfast, wakes up her daughter, and the three of them say a family morning prayer.

Krimion is irate that he has failed to cause dysfunction in the Johnson household. He storms out of the house and levitates high in the air and lets out a roar of anger. The clouds respond to his resentment and turn dark and gray. The sun is blotted out, and rain begins to pour. Krimion commands the wind to blow with precipitous speed. He continues to belt outcries of rage. Each shout causes lightning to strike from the clouds. One lightning bolt strikes a private house, another strikes a phone poll, causing it to collapse on top of a parked car. Heavy rain, along with lightning and thunder ravage throughout this section of Brooklyn. A group of pedestrians run for cover underneath a storefront awning. Krimion causes a bolt of lightning to hit the canopy and fall flat on top of the walkers. Two of them die immediately, while the others are severely injured. Krimion isn't done with his moment of terror. Another jolt of lightning bolts into the ground of a busy middle intersection, causing a three-car accident. A thirteen-year-old girl, sitting in the back of her father's car dies of a broken neck, as her body was thrust forward into the back of the front-side passenger seat. She was not wearing her seatbelt.

"JJ, I'm going to get you! Shouts Krimion.

"Um, please don't call him JJ. He doesn't like to be called JJ."

"Huh, what, who is that?"

"My sheep know my voice," responds the invisible speaker."

"Your sheep do what? Who is this? Wait a minute. Jesus, is that you? And where are you?"

"Yes, it's me. Where am I, you ask? Well, I'm in Canada, Aruba, North Korea, and Saudi Arabia, Jupiter. I'm everywhere, Krimion. You know this already, or have you forgotten? Anyway, do not refer to my son as JJ. His name is Joseph."

Krimion is frightened at the voice of Jesus.

"Ok, fine. I won't call him JJ. Is that the only reason you're here, or have you come to end my flash of fury?"

"Oh no, not at all. Not this time at least. I just came to tell you to show some respect to my servant and refer to him as Joseph, Joseph Johnson, Mr. Johnson, or Pastor Johnson. You can carry on with your little temper tantrum though. I have some other things to tend to. So you continue doing what you're doing here. I'll be.....well, I'll be everywhere. See you soon, Krimion."

"See me soon, you say. Don't you see what I'm am doing to your precious earthlings? Many of them have been killed in a matter of seconds?"

"Oh, I'm aware of their deaths. I'm not too worried though. Well, I don't mind staying here and chatting with you, but I see that I am distracting you from tormenting my people. So, goodbye, Krimion."

"Wait, don't go, Jesus."

69

And with that, the presence of Jesus was no longer in the area.

"Why doesn't he care about his people?" Asks Krimion to himself. "Why would he allow me to raise havoc on the humans? He truly doesn't care. No, that isn't true either. He's playing mind games with me. Damn you, Jesus. You've messed up my train of thought. This is not over, Jesus. Not over at all!"

The Couples Disposition

She waits for her husband to leave the house. She calls her friend and informs him that her husband is gone for the day. Together they plot for a moment to remember.

"So here's the deal, she says. I want to do this now. I can't let another day go by without doing this with you. We can do it today at the church. Meet me in the basement, around 1 pm. This is when Joseph is usually up to preach."

"Okay, I'll see you then." Says the male voice on the other end of the phone conversation. "We have to be discreet with this. If anyone sees us together, they'll know something is up. Should I bring protection or do you have your own."

"I have my own, answers the women, but bring yours as well. A man should always have protection. You can never be too safe."

"Okay, I'll do the same. I really can't wait to do this with you. I've wanted this for a long time. Every time our paths crossed, I could tell that you weren't satisfied. I wanted so bad to step in and fill that void, but your husband was a hindrance. He's a nice guy, and I hate the fact that we're about to do something like this behind his back, but I just can't help it anymore."

"You know what we're about to do is wrong on so many levels." She responds.

"I know it is." Replies the man. "But this is something I want to do. Look, I gotta go. Someone's coming. See you soon."

It is now 12:50 p.m. and Followers of Christ Christian church is packed to capacity. The adult choir sings an original song written by Joseph, entitled *"Jesus is my back up."*

When the choir was done singing, Joseph got up to the pulpit to deliver his sermon. Everyone turns their attention to Pastor Joseph. His presence always commanded the attention of those around. Ten

71

minutes into his address and Willow excuses herself to run downstairs to the ladies' room.

Down in the basement, close to where the kitchen is located, are the voices of a male and female giggling softly?

"Ssh, ssh," says the male voice.

"Okay okay. I'm sorry, but this is fun. Dangerous and fun." Replies the female voice. As fun as this might be, we can't enjoy this for much longer. Now hurry up and do what you gotta do."

"I wanna savor this moment a little bit. Don't you know how long I've wanted to do this with you?"

"Yes I know, but we gotta be cautious. Okay, I think it's wet enough now! Come on, give it to me!"

Ten minutes pass by, and Willow runs back into the sanctuary and hollers out,

"Fire, fire! There's a fire in the building. Everybody get out now!"

Smoke can now be seen at the back of the church. The fire had ascended from the basement to the inside front-doors of the sanctuary. The smoke is slowly filling up the building.

"Everybody to the ground." Yells out Joseph from the pulpit. "Stay low and remain calm."

The crowd of 60,000 plus members are in a state of panic. There are two emergency exits to the left and right of the sanctuary. One of the Deacons attempts to open the door to the right, but the door handle scorches his hand.

72

"Aahhh!" He screams.

The fire is spreading to the outside of the door. Another deacon tries the door on the left side of the church. Without even touching the knob, he can tell that the fire is spread to that side as well.

"Why aren't the sprinklers going off?" Yells someone. "We're trapped. We're all going to die."

It's mayhem inside of FOC. The doors at the sanctuary's entrance are wooden and the fanning fire powers its way inside. It is rushing through the room.

"Quick, everyone run to the back. There's an exit behind the pulpit as well." Joseph says urgently.

The backdoor is a single metal door with multiple locks. Joseph is letting people out one by one. The fire continues to spread and is drawing ferociously to the back. Several members have managed to escape, but the inferno has caught others. Willow runs up to Joseph as he stands by the door.

"Baby you made it." He says with relief.

"Yes, I did Joseph. Where is Willa?"

"I think she got out I wasn't paying attention. So much is going on. Go outside and see if you can find her. I'll go back and see if she's in there somewhere."

Willow runs outside shouting her daughter's name.

"Willa, Willa! Are you out here? If you can hear me, shout yes mommy!"

73

Meanwhile, Joseph is back inside the church, close to the heart of the fire. He shouts for his daughter.

"Willa, Willa. Can you hear me?"

At the same time, Joseph can hear the pain and agony of men, women, and children being burned alive by the fire. He can barely see as the room is black with smoke. He starts coughing and is running out of breath. Realizing that there is little he can do, he runs out of the sanctuary and heads outside.

A majority of the members survived, but 8,000 members didn't make it out alive. The fire department arrives and does their best to put off the fire.

Willow and Joseph continue to call for their daughter. They're hoping that among the 52,000 survivors, one of them is their daughter.

Joseph is losing his mind.

"Willa! Has anyone seen Willa? Brother Johnson, have you seen Willa?"

"No pastor, I haven't."

"Sister Clancy, have you seen my daughter?"

"No pastor, I haven't. Have you seen my husband? He's missing too."

"No sister, I haven't seen him either. Let's pray that they both turn up."

Two hours pass by and all the survivors have been accounted for, but Willa is not one of them. The fire department was still in damage control and was not able to let anyone inside of the building. However, they are taking out dead bodies and handing them to the ambulance. Willow sees a fireman bringing out a small, lifeless little body.

"Joseph, I think I see Willa."

They both run to the fireman. It's Willa.

"My baby, my baby," screams Willow in despair. Is she alive?" She asks the fireman."

"I'm sorry ma'am, she didn't make it. She wasn't burnt much, but she died of smoke inhalation."

Joseph quickly grabs the body and starts crying over his dead child. She's wearing the same turquoise dress that she wore on her birthday; on the day she had her first seizure. Willow drops to the ground wailing with emotion. In desperation, Joseph starts praying to God to revive his daughter. He tries to command Willa back to life. Joseph shakes Willa's body and slaps her face.

"Wake up, Willa! Wake up!" he cries out. Willa is still lifeless. He tries mouth to mouth resuscitation, but no response. Willa is gone.

A wretched Willow wails on the floor.

"Not my baby!" Cries Willow. "Jesuuuuuss! Why, Jesus? Why?" Hatred starts to fill her heart. "Whoever did this, I hope you rot in hell!"

The scene outside of FOC is one of agony and despair. The surviving members of FOC can be seen laid out on the ground as they mourn the loss of their loved ones.

Krimion watches from a distance in approval and playfully responds to Willow's comment.

"You're too late, Willow. I'm already in hell. Soon, your precious little husband will be there as well."

He continues to admire his craftiness in creating a devastating fire.

"Look at what I've done," boasts the maniacal demon. "I did better than I even planned. All I really wanted to do was burn down the church. Having Willa killed was just a bonus. Soon, Joseph will be in hell with Satan. And soon I will be Satan's number two."

"Not bad, Krimion. You killed a lot of people today."

Krimion looks around to see who is talking to him.

"Satan, is that you?"

"My sheep know my voice, Krimion."

"Jesus, it's you again! Why are you tormenting me?"

"Wait a minute here," responds Jesus. "So you're the one causing a fire that has killed 8000 people and I'm the tormentor?"

"I'm only doing my job. Have you come to send me back to hell?"

"No, not at all. You'll be sent back sooner than you think. I'm just admiring your work. It's pretty good. Too bad you chose to go the evil route. You would have made an excellent commander in my army. But you elected to side with Satan. I mean, he did make you think that he was going to lead you to the forbidden universe. And look how that has panned out for you all. But hey, don't let that discourage you from your current endeavors. You're doing a marvelous job with your nettlesome tactics on Joseph. But I digress. I'm going to leave you be, and let you continue with your plan to lure Joseph. As you were."

Jesus once again disappears from Krimion. An angry and confused Krimion doesn't know how to ascertain Jesus' momentary appearance.

"Why does he continue to trouble me about this boy Joseph? Shouldn't one of his angels be down here trying to battle me? He's messing with my head again. I need to just forget about him for now, and enjoy today's disaster."

As Krimion goes back to admire his work, detective Shapiro of the 23rd precinct shows up and takes witness statements and pictures of the church. A distraught Joseph and Willow barely have enough strength to speak to the detective. Realizing that everyone is in mourning, the detective takes the phone number of Joseph and agrees to reach out to him in a day or two.

All in all, this is a day that the media would call, *the fire at followers.*

The next day, Mr. Resnick hears about the fire and immediately calls Joseph to offer his condolences.

"Joseph, words cannot fully express my sympathy for you, your family, and your congregation. Please send my condolences to your members."

"Thanks, Alex. My wife and I are devastated, as are many of our members. We lost a lot of people yesterday. Adults and children. The church is practically ruined.

"Not completely Joseph. I am offering you my resources in the restoration of your church. I will assign my men to help bring your church back to what it was, perhaps even better."

"Oh wow, Alex. That's mighty generous of you, but I can't ask you to do that. You've already done way too much for me as it is."

"Nonsense, Joseph. You're not asking; I'm offering. This will be free of charge. No expense will be spared. By the help of God, you will have your church up and running in a few months. But in the meantime, I have a catering hall just about a mile from your church. I'll rent that place out to you and your member's until the restoration of the church is completed."

"My goodness, Alex. That is beyond kind. How can I ever repay you?"

"You just keep doing what you're doing in this neighborhood and that will be payment enough. As for now, I need you to stop by the Synagogue next week Thursday and we'll discuss renovation plans.

A week has passed by since the fire, with funerals services for the deceased having been completed over the past five days. The members of FOC are still in disbelief over the loss of their loved ones. Joseph and Willow have lost their precious Willa. Joseph has been praying to God, asking him for an explanation for this tragedy. He has been faithful to God over these past eight years. He never wavered in

78

his commitment to God. Always focused on living an exemplary and faithful life to his God. So he wondered why God would allow this to happen to him. Nevertheless, even though he questioned God, he still gave his Lord the benefit of the doubt and continued to praise and worship his savior.

Thursday comes, and Joseph makes his way to the Synagogue to speak with Alex. As he approaches the temple, he walks inside but doesn't see or hear anyone. He then walks over to the left and sees a stained-glass door to an office partially open. Inside the room are Alex, his wife Rita, and Rabbi Shapiro. As he walks over, he is about to announce himself, but he then hears his name uttered and stays back to listen in on the conversation.

"I don't understand why we have to help out Joseph and his church. They have plenty of members who are capable to financially assist with the renovation."

"Rita, my Love, responds Alex. Joseph is my friend. He is a good guy, with good people. They have suffered a great loss. The least we can do is bless them with our labor."

"Good people, you say. Didn't one of his good people assault you just a few blocks from here?"

"Yes, Rita. But that is old news. We must learn to forgive if we're going to be a striving community."

"I'm sorry Alex, but I'm gonna have to agree with your wife here," Interjects the Rabbi. "Let them fend for themselves. Besides, they're not God's children. We are! Their so-called Messiah supposedly went back to heaven and hasn't returned in over 2000 years to establish his kingdom. Their religion is fake."

79

"Well, at least their Messiah came. We're still waiting for ours to make his first appearance. So based on your argument, Judaism should be considered faker than Christianity."

"How dare you speak ill of our faith! Reacts the Rabbi.

"I am not speaking ill of anything. I am merely showing you how wrong your point on Christianity truly is. But all this is beside the point. The issue today is whether or not to help Joseph and his brethren. And with or without your blessings, I am going to help him."

Joseph has had enough of the eavesdropping and hollers out, "Hello! Anyone here?"

Alex opens the door with a smile on his face.

"Here we are, Joseph. Come on in. We were just talking about you. My wife, the Rabbi, and I were just discussing how pleased we are to assist you and your members in rebuilding your church. Isn't that right, Rita?"

Rita begrudgingly walks out of the room, speaking Yiddish, in disagreement with Alex's decision.

"Was it something I said?" Asks Joseph.

"Pay her no mind." Responds the Rabbi. "Rita is just in a bad mood."

"Oh, okay, just checking. Listen, if assisting me in restructuring my church is going to be a physical or financial hassle on your people, then I would understand if you backed out of your promise."

"Listen here, Joseph. In Jewish custom, it is wrong to back out of a promise. When a Jew makes a promise, he is bound to fulfill that promise. But even if it weren't wrong, I still wouldn't back out. I am going to help you whether you like it or not."

Aware that Mrs. Resnick and the Rabbi were apprehensive about this deal, Joseph plays ignorant but still agrees.

"Well, once again, I must say thank you all for your generosity. My members will want to return this act of kindness in the same way down the road."

And with that, Alex and Joseph work out the details of the renovation.

Exorcising His Power

Three months pass, and FOC is ready for the re-opening of their church inside the Riley Arena. The Sanctuary is as beautiful as ever. New stain-glass windows, shining chandeliers, along with a top-notch sound system are just a few of the new and apparent additions to the church. Also added to the church are ten state of the art security cameras stationed in and outside various parts of the church. Alex upgraded the building's sprinkler system as well.

During these past three months, Joseph had been fasting and praying aggressively. His members followed suit and did the same. The survivors from the fire at Followers had become mentally and spiritually stronger since the horrific incident and are ready for the re-coronation of their place of worship.

On this Sunday morning, all the members are decked out in their Sunday best. Joseph declared that today is to be a day of Jubilee. From the little babes to the eldest members, the members of FOC are going to sing, dance, and shout as if they've just won the Super Bowl.

Service starts with the choir singing one of Joseph's favorite hymns – *Death hath no terror*. Praise dancers are dancing through the aisles. Everyone in the pews is on their feet singing and dancing along. Joseph and Willow stand side by side on the pulpit, praising and thanking God for blessing them in spite of all that has happened. Today is a glorious day in the house of the Lord

After about 30 minutes of singing, scripture readings, and testimonies. Joseph walks to the podium to deliver his sermon for the day.

As he starts to preach, in walks Karen with her son. She quietly sits in the back of the church and listens to the father of her child preach with eloquence and command.

Twelve minutes pass by, and Krimion makes his way inside the sanctuary and stands next to Karen. He whispers in her ear.

"Do it."

She says, "No, I can't."

He replies. "Yes, you can. You deserve answers."

"It would be wrong to do it now."

"Now is the time! Do it! Before you miss your opportunity."

Karen has no idea that a demon is speaking to her. She thinks that she is having a conversation with herself. Karen never accepted Jesus Christ as her savior nor has she been spiritually awakened to the forces of darkness.

She gets up from her seat.

"Favor, you stay right here. Mommy will be right back."

Karen walks down the aisle and has now caught the attention of Joseph and the entire congregation.

Joseph takes a pause from his sermon to address Karen.

"Is there a problem?"

"Yes!" She shouts. "When are you going to take care of your son?"

The crowd whispers among themselves.

"Son? What son is she talking about?

Joseph is shell-shocked.

"Yes, everyone. Joseph and I share a child together and he is neglecting his duties."

Joseph steps down from the pulpit and walks over the Karen.

"How' bout we go into my office and talk about this in private. No one here needs to be a part of this drama right now."

"Whatever! Let's go then."

"I'm coming too," interrupts Willow. I'm not having some woman locked up in an office with my man."

Joseph then signals one of the Ushers to keep an eye on Favor while the three of them hash things out in the office.

"The three of them get to the office. Willow slams the door and turns to Karen."

"Who the hell do you think you are, barging up in our church in the middle of Joseph's sermon? Don't you have any respect for the house of God?"

"Joseph, get your wife from my face before she gets beat down up in this room."

"Okay ladies. Please settle down and let's act like adults. Everyone have a seat. Now, Karen, I am sorry that I have been neglecting my son. I've been through a lot these past few months. Between this church getting set on fire, and my daughter dying, thinking about taking care of another child was not on my radar."

"Well, he needs to be on your radar now. Your son needs his real father in his life."

"Wait a minute," Interrupts Willow. "Joseph needs proof that he is the father. Ya'll need to get this DNA test done. If this chick cheated on her husband with you, who knows who else she was sleeping with at that time."

"Excuse me," yells Karen. "Just because we're inside of a church does not mean that I won't slap the hell out of you. Don't disrespect me like that."

"Yeah, I'd love to see you try and slap me. Just because I'm dignified doesn't mean I won't get street on you."

"Well, I'm right here, Willow. Whatcha gonna do?"

"That's it. Let go!"

Willow proceeds to take off her earrings, necklace, and her three-inch high-heel shoes. Karen is doing the same. The two of them are talking smack to each other and they are ready to throw hands. Joseph is about to interfere, but something has drawn his attention. He looks over to the right corner of the office and thinks he sees something.

"Ladies. Ladies, what is that in the corner?"

"What are you talking about?" Asks Willow, with one of her shoes in her hand, ready to strike Karen.

"There's an odd-looking figure over there in that corner. It looks like a big piece of stone. Can't you ladies see it?"

"No, we can't," respond to two ladies in unison.

Suddenly, Joseph's spiritual eyes are opened and he can see as clear as day that there is a demon before him. It's Krimion – and he looks as mad as ever.

"My God! Shouts Joseph. Ladies, get behind me."

"Joseph, what is it. You're scaring me," replies a now frantic Karen.

85

"It's a demon. A demon from hell."

"What is this, a joke? How can you see a demon?" Asks Karen, with a slight chuckle.

"Um Karen, Joseph wouldn't joke about this. If he says he sees a demon, I assure you, he sees a demon."

"That's right Willow. This demon is real. He's the one responsible for all the drama going on with me. He caused Willa's seizures, he caused the fire, and he brought Karen here today to start a fight. But today, it's time to face my devil. Joseph's devil."

And with a loud voice, Joseph yells, "Get out!"

Krimion can't believe that a human has spotted him. So he crawls on the walls in a semi-retreat. Joseph runs toward Krimion, and shouts out again, "Get out!"

Krimion shouts back. "No, I'm going to kill you!"

Karen and Willow are now standing on top of a couch, holding on to each other as if they are best buddies. Like a spider, Krimion is running all over the ceiling and walls of the office, trying to attack Joseph.

Again, Joseph shouts "Get out of here, you demon." But Krimion is resistant to Joseph's demands and continues to crawl along the office walls. Joseph doesn't know what to do to. Then his mind goes back to when Willa was alive, and she experienced her second seizure inside of the church. He recalls Mother Berry casting out a demon while speaking in tongues. He rushes over to the demon, pulls out his crucifix and shouts, "demon from hell, I know your name. Your name is Krimion. You're the same demon that mother Berry sent away when you gave my daughter another seizure in church. The spirit of God has now revealed this to me. And today, at this moment in time, in the name of Jesus Christ, I cast you away from this place and back to your place of resting."

Immediately, Krimion vanishes away from the church.

"Is it gone, Joseph." Asks Karen.

"Yes, Karen. My devil is gone. But he'll be back. And next time he'll return stronger and more determined to bring discord to my loved ones and me."

"My God, Joseph. I knew that you were anointed by God, and have done many miraculous things in the past, but you visually being able to see a demon and to cast him out, is as spiritual as one can get."

"Well, Karen these are the things that God has allowed me to see from time to time. But to be honest, we can all see within the spirit realm if we completely turn our lives to the Lord. Karen, I strongly suggest that you accept Jesus Christ as your Lord and Savior and that you get baptized immediately."

"Yes, Joseph. I definitely am a believer today. I'll get baptized whenever you are ready."

"Hallelujah." Shouts Joseph. "The demon thought that by bringing you here, that you would cause dysfunction within my home and my church, but God had a plan all along, and now another person is being added to his kingdom. Karen, I promise to take care of my son. Willow, I still love you, and I don't want you to feel threatened or concerned about this new bond that Karen and I now share."

"Okay, Joseph. I trust you, and I suppose I can learn to trust Karen. But what are we going to tell the congregation upstairs?"

"We'll tell them exactly what happened. Verbatim!" Explains Joseph. "We'll tell them how the two of you were arguing. We'll tell them how I saw a demon watching from within this room. And I'll explain to them that I sent the demon away, and now Karen is ready to be baptized. I won't sugarcoat a thing! I'll tell them about my affair with Karen prior to my marriage and that I just recently learned about my son with her. They'll feel a little bit funny about the whole scenario, but eventually, they will come around. Are you two ladies with me on this?"

The two ladies nod their heads in agreement. All three of them now head back up to the sanctuary where Joseph explains everything in detail to his members. Just as he suspects, the members are thrown off by Joseph's pre-marital affair, but they immediately forgive him and embrace him, his wife, and their newest member, Karen.

Satanic Eruption

Krimion is back at the throne of Satan, frightened to be back in his master's presence.

"Krimion, what are you doing here, and where is Joseph?"

88

"My Lord, my apologies to you, but he is not here. He saw me. Joseph saw me with his own two eyes. He then banished me from his presence, in the name of Jesus."

"How did you manage to let him see you?"

"I don't know my Lord. I was in his office, watching his wife and his son's mother argue. I was simply admiring the drama that was about to unfold. I don't know how, but he saw me lurking in the corner and addressed me. He even knew my name."

"You idiot! Why were you lurking around him? He's highly sensitive to the spiritual realm. He's not your typical blind-faith Christian. God actually speaks to him. And now he has just exorcised you from his presence."

"My Lord, I promise this won't happen again. Next time I'll be more cau...."

But before Krimion can finish his sentence, Satan grabs him by his two feet and starts to swing his servant from left to right, slamming him to the ground.

"My Lord, please I beg you, have mercy on me."

"Shut up, you buffoon. You're becoming a complete waste of my time." Satan says as he continuously pounds Krimion to the ground. The pounding causes disruption within the volcano, as acid starts to erupt.

"My lord, please stop. This place is about to explode."

Satan ignores Krimion's plea for mercy. He throws Krimion from one wall of the volcano to another. And before Krimion can muster enough strength to get to his feet, Satan rushes over to him and ferociously throws him back to the other side of the walls. This constant banging against the walls of the volcano is causing the larva to rise higher. Satan takes Krimion by the feet again and ascends out of the volcano. And Like a baseball player at batting practice, he swings Krimion with aggressive force on the outer walls of the volcano. Four, five, and six times, he does this. The larva continues to erupt out of the volcano due to the pounding it is receiving from Krimion's body. Not only that but the vibration from Krimion getting swung onto the volcano so many times, is forming a severe Tsunami. Residents in nearby villages are fleeing for safety, as water surges on land from the Pacific Ocean. The residents run for their lives, attempting to go as far inland as possible. Unfortunately, many of them do not survive. The surge of water is destroying many homes. Power lines fall into the water, causing many to be electrocuted to death. Debris from homes and businesses injure and kill many residents. While this is going on, the Prince of Darkness continues to torment Joseph's Devil. In a matter of seconds, he takes Krimion several miles in the air at an accelerated pace. And with the same speed, he descends through the sky, deep diving into the Pacific Ocean. While within the deep blue waters of the Ocean, Satan rapidly punches his subject in the face.

As Satan finishes punishing Krimion for getting cast away by Joseph, he re-ascends back into the sky, still with Krimion in his arms. He looks over the devastation he has caused and gloats about it to Krimion.

"See, this is how you torment people. This is how you destroy lives. This is how you make them deny God. While the government will be sending their thoughts and prayers, the residents will be left to fend for themselves. Many of them are Christians with equal to, if not greater than, spiritual gifts than Joseph. So I want you to go back to Joseph and make him deny his God. I want you to torment the hell out of him. I want you to make his life a living hell, and then bring him to me in this hell!"

"Yes, my lord. I will go back to him right away. Let me get my things, and I'll be on my way."

"No you won't, you idiot! Whenever a Christian casts a demon away, that demon is stuck in wherever he was cast for at least 48 hours. So you can stay your rock-headed-self down here for a little while, and clean up this mess you made me create."

"Yes, my king. As you wish."

So Krimion stays on the Pacific coast, where he mulls over his plots and plans for Joseph.

Surveillance Says?

It is now two days later since Karen showed up at Joseph's church. Joseph is in his car driving home after spending some time at the church. His phone rings. It's detective Flacco. Joseph pulls over to answer his phone.

"Good afternoon, detective! How can I help you?"

"Pastor Joseph, I'm sitting here in my office and I think I have a crack in the case of your church fire."

"That's great! So what's the crack?"

"I have some video surveillance that you might wanna look at."

"But detective, my church didn't have any cameras in our building at the time."

"You're right, Pastor. But there's a little bodega across the street from your church. That store has two cameras and of them directly faces your building. There's something in the video that you need to see. Can you come down to the station now?"

"Sure I can, let me just go home and get my wife. Be there in about an hour."

"No, come alone. I don't want too many faces looking at this video just yet."

"Okay, detective. Whatever you say. I'll be there in an hour or so."

Joseph races home to get a quick bite to eat. He's curious to know exactly what's on the video. He reaches his home in twelve minutes and double parks his car. As he does on many occasions, he enters his house through the backyard. By this time, Willow is generally in the kitchen with dinner prepared. But today, she's not. He proceeds to walk up the stairs when he hears his wife talking to someone on the phone while in her bedroom. He stays hidden away, to listen to what she is saying.

"This is all my fault! Look at the damage I've caused. This is too far. We've definitely crossed the line. And now God is going to punish us. What we did was wrong, and I don't think there is anything we can say or do to undo the damage. If it weren't for me, Willa would probably be alive today. But it is what it is. We have to move forward somehow and tell no one what we've done."

Joseph can't believe the words he hears coming from his wife's mouth.

"What does she mean by 'Willa would be alive today'? I don't understand. Could my wife be responsible for the fire?"

Joseph no longer wants to listen in on the conversation, so he makes two hard steps up the stairs to alert Willow that he has arrived. Willow quickly pretends as if she is talking to someone else.

"Okay, Sarah. I'll talk to you later, girl."

Willow then looks over to the bedroom door and sees her husband walking in.

"Hey, Joseph. Are you hungry? I'll have some food for you in a minute."

"Yeah I'll have a quick bite, but then I have to head back out. I have to get to the precinct. The detective has some information vital to the fire."

"Oh, that's great. Did he tell you what information he has?"

"Yes, he said that he has video surveillance from outside of the church."

"What video surveillance?" Our church didn't have any surveillance at that time."

"True, but the little bodega across the street has one. I'm heading to the police station now to see who or what is in that video."

"Okay great. I'll come along; I'm curious to see who might have been responsible for this fire."

"No, Willow, you can't come. The detective told me not to bring anyone."

"Well, this is preposterous!" said an infuriated Willow. "That church is just as much mine as it is yours."

"Don't worry, Willow; I'll be sure to keep you abreast to what I find out. I'm sure the detective is just being extra cautious."

Joseph said all this knowing that he overheard his wife making suspicious remarks over the phone to someone about the fire. But as much as what he heard bothered him, he didn't want to jump to any conclusions.

"All right, Joseph. You go ahead to the police precinct. I'll go run some errands, as well as have dinner ready by the time you return."

Joseph leaves for the precinct. Willow gets back on her phone and dials the person she was last speaking to.

"Hello, Brian."

"Yeah, what's up?"

"We have a major problem. The police have informed Joseph that there was videotape outside the church the day of the fire. Joseph is heading there now to view the video."

"Shoot! This is not good. Not good at all. I'm going to be in a lot of trouble if I am seen on that tape. I should leave town. Ya know, lay low for a bit."

"Lay low! Oh no, If I'm going down, you're going down too."

"We could run away together, Willow."

"I'm going to pretend I didn't hear that, Brian. Joseph does not deserve to be abandoned; not after all he's been through. Brian just stay cool. Let's see what the video shows before we start any evacuation procedures."

"Willow this whole ordeal has me nervous." He says while pacing back and forth throughout his house. "Can you imagine the repercussions for our actions? Oh no, I have too much to lose. I'm leaving town today. You can join me if you want, but I'm leaving town in the next four hours, with or without you."

Willow has now lost her patience with the babbling idiot. She wishes she was in his presence so that she could slap some calm into him.

"Brian Gimber!" She yells. "Would you shut up and man up! Stop freaking out and do not make any impulsive decisions. Don't you know that running away implies guilt? Now stop being a sissy and let me handle everything. You just act normal until I contact you again."

"Okay, okay. You're right." He says as he exhales heavily. "I do need to calm down and let things play out a little bit. But if we get

95

caught, I can forget about running for City Council, and I can forget about having a normal life."

"Don't worry, Brian. You will become the next City Council!" She says emphatically. "I'll make sure of that. Anyway, I gotta go. Keep your cell phone on you at all times. I may need to call you again with an update."

Back at the Precinct, Detective Flacco is with Joseph. He sets up the video recording at around 12:30 PM. He fast forwards two minutes later and sees a brown-skinned male running away from the church with haste. The man is running as if he is running away from something or someone.

"Wait, wait, Detective. Rewind that a few seconds."

"Why? Do you recognize the man?"

"Yeah, that's Brian Gimber. He's a member of my church. He's a good guy, but why is he running?"

"That's what I'd like to know." Responds the Detective. "Something sure seems fishy about this. But tell me, Joseph, do you have any Caucasian members in your church?"

"Well yes, we have about fifteen Caucasian members; Children included. But the majority of our members are black Americans or from the Caribbean."

"So check this out, Pastor. Out walks an elderly man and woman. Both Caucasian. Do you recognize them?"

"I can't tell. The video isn't clear."

"No worries. I can zoom in the picture for you. Is that better?"

Joseph's mouth opens wide in dismay.

"What? What is it? Asks the detective."

"That's Rabbi and Mrs. Resnick."

"Oh, so they're Jewish. What are two Jewish people doing coming out of your church?"

"Well Mrs. Resnick's husband, Alex, is the one who sold me the building. He paid for most of the expenses in the rebuilding. I met the Rabbi some weeks ago when Alex, that is, Mr. Resnick offered to pay for the remodeling of the church and the rebuilding. My guess is that they were there to see how the church looked."

"Joseph, you said that you met the Rabbi. Tell me, did he seem like a nice person? Did he seem as if he didn't like you?"

"I mean I do recall having a strange vibe with him. Oh yeah, I just remembered. One time I overheard the Rabbi, Mr. Resnick, and Mrs. Resnick talking. Mrs. Resnick and the Rabbi were apprehensive about Mr. Resnick providing me with his services for the church. Also, I should mention that one of my younger members attacked Mr. Resnick in the street over a disagreement. But once I heard about the incident, I reprimanded the young man. He didn't take it too well and started spewing out anti-Semitic slurs. Slurs that I dare not say out loud to you."

"My goodness, Joseph! Between Mrs. Resnick, the Rabbi, and Brian Gimber, we have three persons of interest in this fire investigation. I'll be contacting all three of them for questioning."

"Well, do what you gotta do, detective. I don't believe that any of these three persons is capable of deliberately starting a fire. But I'll let you do your job. Is that all for today, detective?"

97

"Yes, Joseph. I'll be contacting you as more information is provided."

Joseph and the detective part ways, with Joseph wondering if Brian actually did start the fire. Brian has been a loyal member of Followers of Christ since its inception. Whenever Joseph needed something done at the church, Brian was always ready and willing to assist. If Joseph had to stay late at the church to counsel someone, Brian always made sure that Willow and Willa got home safe. Joseph could call Brian at Two O'clock in the morning, and Brian would be there to assist Joseph in whatever he needed.

Now Mrs. Resnick and the Rabbi, Joseph does not trust. The day they all met up at the synagogue, Joseph realized that the Rabbi and Mrs. Resnick weren't too fond of him. Joseph sensed a certain level of hatred and a certain degree of evil. But he can't fathom that their hatred for Joseph, Christianity, or for that matter, black people, to be at such an apex, that they would find themselves scheming to burn down a place of worship.

All in all, Joseph drives home a confused man.

Ten minutes later and Joseph arrives at his home. Coming through the front door is the scent of a delicious home-cooked meal. Willow had prepared an elegant supper for Joseph. Risotto, macaroni, and cheese, with veal cutlet, are on today's menu.

Joseph walks into the dining room, to an already set table.

"Mmm mmm, this room smells good."

Willow smiles in satisfaction at Joseph's observant expression.

98

"You must be starving," she says. "C'mon, sit down and eat. Tell me what you learned from the detective."

"Okay baby, but you have a seat and let me dish out your plate for you. That's the least I could do after you've been slaving in the kitchen."

"Well, thank you. I wouldn't mind getting served for a change."

Joseph pulls out a chair from under the dining room table, and gestures for Willow to sit. As willow sits down, Joseph smoothly pushes in her seat to a comfortable position to the table. Joseph then blesses the food and starts dishing out his wife's plate. Willow is nervous as a suspected criminal called in by the police for questioning. Her legs are shivering. Her knees periodically clang, while her heart beats with rapid speed.

"So go ahead Joseph, tell me what you learned today."

He pours himself a cup of tea, adding sugar and stirring methodically. He blows into his spoon and before taking a sip, he says, "Today, I learned not to associate with sneaky people."

Willow's anxiety accelerates.

"Oh yeah?" she says. "And who are these sneaky people?"

"Brian Gimber. Back-stabbing Brian. He's seen in the video running away from the church just moments before the fire spread to the sanctuary."

"Wait a minute Joseph. This doesn't mean that he knew anything about the fire. Maybe he had an emergency somewhere and had to leave. That video is not enough proof."

99

"Perhaps you're right. I shouldn't be so quick to cast judgment. It's just that I've always had this bad vibe about Brian. I know that he's a good guy and all, but he seems like the type of guy who would kill a child if it meant saving his own skin. Willow, you grew with this man. Is he trustworthy, or should I be concerned?"

"My goodness, yes, he's trustworthy. Brian would never hurt a fly."

"Okay, if you say so. Anyway, there's more to the video."

"Really! What else did you see?"

"I saw Mrs. Resnick and the Rabbi walking out of the church a few minutes after Brian."

"What! You saw Mrs. Resnick and the Rabbi walking out of our church! Joseph, it's gotta be them. They're the arsonists. You and I both know that Mrs. Resnick had never set foot in our church before – even when we were located at the store-front. And the Rabbi was with her also? Their dislike for the black American community is obvious. If Alex was with them, then I could probably say that they were visiting. But there's no way that those two alone would come to our church for no reason. Grand re-opening or not!"

"Willow, there's definitely a possibility that they started the fire. Detective Flacco will be calling them in for questions, as well as Brian. But I just want to know why anyone would want to burn down our church. Hopefully, we'll get some answers soon."

"I hope so, Joseph. I want us to be able to put this behind us once and for all."

"Me too Willow. Oh, one more thing. During the fire, I recall seeing Brian go downstairs minutes after you went downstairs. Did you happen to run into him?"

"Hmm. I'm sorry. It has been a while now. I can't say that I remember at this time. My guess is that he went to the restroom before he ran off in a hurry."

Joseph is now about to question Willow about the secret phone conversations she been having, and the suspiciousness behind them. But his phone rings. He looks to see who is calling him. His face brightens up. It's Karen. Willow notices the look of life in his eyes when Joseph realized who was calling. Joseph quickly catches himself and answers the phone as if he is being bothered.

"Hello, Karen. How may I help you?"

"Hi, Joseph. You don't have to answer the phone like a customer service rep, ya know. Is this a bad time? I can call you back later."

"Oh, I'm sorry about that. I just have a lot going on. The investigation into the church fire is pickup up speed, so my wife and I are a little on edge. Is there something that I can do for you?"

"Not me exactly, but Favor wanted to spend some time with you. Are you free for a couple of hours of father-son time today?"

"Of course I'm free to see my son."

Joseph now covers his phone and whispers to Willow that Favor is coming over to spend some time with him.

101

This has somewhat placed Willow in a sour mood. She was looking forward to making love with her husband immediately after dinner. She wants to give Joseph a son they could share. She now fears that Joseph will be content with having Favor in his life. Nevertheless, she doesn't express any hatred for Favor or Karen. She did not want to sound like the jealous, over-protective wife. So in a gesture of false exuberance, she gives Joseph a smile and two thumbs up as a sign of acceptance.

Twenty minutes pass by, and Karen arrives with her son. Favor's resemblance to Joseph in unearthing. Joseph greets Karen with a friendly hug. He then stoops down and hugs his son.

"Hi young man, you wanna go in the backyard and play catch?"

Favor nods his head up and down.

"Now, Favor, that's not how we address people, remember? You have to speak words." Says his mom.

"I'm sorry, mommy. Yes, daddy. Let's play catch!"

Joseph and Favor head to the backyard. The two women sit in the living room, across from each other and are avoiding eye contact. Karen wants to make conversation, while Willow is counting down the time for Karen and Favor to leave.

Karen scans her eyes over the living-room.

"This is a nice place you have here, Willow."

Willow rolls her eyes, crosses her legs, and with a soft undertone voice, she says, "I know."

Karen, realizing that Willow is not opening up for dialogue, makes a second attempt at conversation.

"So how long have you guys been here?"

Willow is done with the small talk.

"Look here, girlie, if you think that you're going to swoop in and take my husband away from me just because you have a son together, you better think again."

"I don't want your man, all right! I just want my son to have a relationship with his father."

"Oh is that all you want?" Snaps Willow. "I'm not dumb, you know. I know how ya'll baby mama's act. You'll find any reason to call the father. Saying, my son needs this, my son needs that. My son wants you to come over and tell him a bed-time story. That's when you'll try to lure him into bed with you."

"Someone here watches way too much T.V. Look, I get that you would feel a little insecure."

"Insecure? Insecure? I am far from insecure. Joseph has a smart, sexy, and independent wife. He doesn't need a woman like you in his life. Look at you. You cheated on your husband with Joseph, and then you hid your son from Joseph."

"Well then you should be thanking me because had I told him that he was the father back then, he would have never married you."

"You know what, Karen? I think it's time for you to leave."

"Oh, I ain't going nowhere; at least not today, that is."

"You know what? I'm just going to call Joseph and tell him that his little father-son time is over."

Willow gets up off her couch to talk to Joseph. Karen jumps up from the sofa and stands in front of Willow.

"Girl, if you don't get from in front of me, there's going to be hell to pay."

"Willow, if you go anywhere near Joseph, I'll tell him about the handsome young man you were having sex with the day of the fire."

A startled Willow backs away. Her eyes survey the room as she looks for an object to strike Karen. She changes her mind and sits back down on the couch.

"You're probably wondering how I would know such a thing. Well, I'll tell ya. I was at the church during the fire. My son wasn't with me that time. I wanted to talk to Joseph about our son. I got to the church around the time he started to preach. I decided to head downstairs to the ladies room to freshen up a bit. When I got downstairs, I heard soft whispering. I debated whether to go pee or to track down the mysterious voices. I decided on the former. I mean, I really had to pee. So after I finished using the ladies room, I walked through the halls to see if I could locate the voices. I could have sworn that the first voice was that of a white person with a bit of an accent, but I was mistaken. I definitely heard the voice of a black woman. Anyway, as I walked down the basement hall, which is beautiful by the way, I found myself at the door of the boiler room. I cracked the door ever so slightly and watched as you and some man not named Joseph, have sex. So you can say whatever you want about me, but you my friend, are boiler room trash!"

104

"You bitch! Hollers Willow."

"It takes one to know one. You're lucky I didn't take pictures. The only thing that stopped me from taking pictures was that I heard a man and a woman walking my way. They sounded Jewish or maybe Russian. I couldn't quite tell. Anyways, I ran upstairs and went outside. A few minutes later, the fire started."

"So what is it that you want from Joseph and me now that you know that I am cheating on him?"

"I already told you, Willow. I just want Favor to have his daddy in his life. I don't want Joseph. Even though he is a good man and good lover, my true love is out there somewhere."

"So you're not going to tell Joseph that I cheated on him?"

"Only if you give me a reason to. Look I get it. You have your reasons, whatever they may be. Just know that the next time you're in church jumping, shouting, speaking in tongues, it means absolutely nothing to me."

Joseph walks in and sees the two ladies talking. Favor runs up to Karen and tells her all about his time with his dad.

"So you two didn't kill each other, huh?" asks Joseph.

"No. Not at all." Responds Willow.

"Yeah, that's right. Echoes Karen. We came to a mutual understanding."

"That's good to hear; I want all of us to get along. We gotta remember that Satan is busy. He'll use our current situation to his advantage and try to separate us from God. I sense that the devil will be

105

back stronger and more determined. We have got to be smart. We've got to be ready. I have a bad feeling that another storm is coming."

A Blast of Fury

Krimion has been re-strategizing his plans for Joseph. His 48 hours are up, and he is ready to head back to Brooklyn. But just before he is about to leave, Satan stops him.

"Not so fast, idiot! While you were in timeout, I had one of my other subjects check out Joseph and the gang to see what they were up to. Did you know that Karen was there the day of the fire and witnessed Willow and Brian having sex?"

"No, My lord. I wasn't aware."

"That's right Krimion. And now, Karen is holding that over Willow's head. This goes to show you that sometimes less is best. We don't have to meddle in the human's affairs every minute of the day. These fools are capable of sinning on their own. We are just there to, you know, gently nudge them in the wrong direction. Now with that being said, take this new information and use it to your advantage."

"Yes, Satan. This is absolute gold. I'll be sure to rain fire and fury on Joseph and his clan this time around. He is a strong man, but I shall weaken him."

"No need for the fire and fury. Just find Joseph's weakness and use it against him."

Satan begins to reflect on something.

"Krimion, have a seat. Let me tell you the story of how I got Adam and Eve to sin."

"As you know, the Lord commanded his first two humans not to eat of the forbidden fruit. And initially, they were obedient to God's commands. But over time, I noticed that Eve would walk by the tree and glance at it. I could tell that she wished to have just one bite of this desirable fruit. On another occasion, I witnessed Adam lusting after the fruit. I knew it was only a matter of time before one of them caved."

"So one day, I approached one of the snakes in the garden. We made a deal that he would live to regret. I told him that if he lets me possess his body for a period of time, I would inform him of the secrets of God. The snake was intrigued by this offer, as he desired to be the wisest of all the animals. Needless to say, the serpent accepted my offer and I inhabited his body. In the guise of the serpent, I gained easy access to Adam and Eve. One day, while Adam was walking by the

107

tree, I camouflaged my body to the tree and knocked a fruit to the ground. Adam saw it, and I just knew he would take a bite. But no, he didn't. Instead, he took the fruit and buried it underneath the dirt. I got a little frustrated and impatient. But then I observed something about Eve. She was pretty naive for a human. In today's society, one might refer to her as ditzy."

"One day Adam played a trick on Eve. He told her that female humans gain the ability to fly on their sixteenth birthday. So would you believe that when her sixteenth birthday came, this genius is jumping off rocks and flapping her arms, trying to fly? Adam was cracking up. He made Eve feel like such a fool. She stayed mad at him for about two days. But when you're the only two humans on earth, there's only so much silent treatment she could give. But I digress, the fact was that I knew she would believe anything anyone would say to her."

"A week passes by, and she walks by the tree. This time I call her. Eve, Eve! Come and have some delicious fruit."

"You speak," she replied.

"Of course, I do. Now here, have a bite."

"No." She said. "God said I would die the moment I eat the fruit."

"That's not true," I rebutted. "God is keeping secrets from you. He knows that you'll be as wise as him and be like a god when you eat this fruit. Besides, what kind of god dangles a beautiful looking fruit in front of you, just to tell you not to eat of it?"

"Krimion, I tell you that at that moment, I knew that I had her. The moment a person shows even an ounce of doubt about God, you can quickly get that person to turn against him."

"Eve took the fruit, ate it, and gave some to her husband. Adam, still having guilt from the Eve birthday fly joke, ate the fruit as well."

"After that, the innocence of man was gone. Of course, the snake was punished for letting me inhabit him. God then swore that the seed of Eve was going to crush me, but that's neither here nor there."

"So Krimion, have you learned anything from this story?"

"Yes, that because of you and your lies, we're all doomed?"

"No, you buffoon! The moral of the bloody story is that humans will tell you how to handle them just by merely watching them. What's the matter with you and your idiotic answer?"

"So we're not doomed, my lord?"

"What the....Just get out of my presence before I melt down your atrocious looking head. Idiot!"

Krimion scurries away in haste, fearing Satan's frustration will be expressed on him. Krimion is not the patient and methodical type of demon. He prefers instant actions with instant results. He built his resume of tyranny on being aggressive with humans. Sitting back and letting things play out is not his forte. If he were human, he'd probably be diagnosed with ADHD.

As he soars over the Pacific Ocean, he starts to mutter to himself.

109

"Who does Satan think he is? Just because he took down Adam and Eve, he feels that he has a monopoly on the methods of human behavior. Well, I've caused my share of mayhem. The Cuban missile crises; I started that. The Civil War in Rwanda; I started that. Jim Crows laws in America, I started that. So Satan can take his slow-paced tortoise-like strategies, and shove it. I've been successful for centuries, doing things my way. Certainly, I will continue to do things my way. And my way will be the winning way."

So Krimion flies over the Pacific Ocean and over through the heart of the United States. After a few hours of travel, he finally makes his way back to Brooklyn, and in the presence of Joseph.

Saturday has come, and the Resnick's are on their way to the Synagogue for their Sabbath service. It's a beautiful autumn day with the leaves displaying a beautiful crimson color. A light jacket is all one would need, as today's weather is in the mid-60s.

As usual, the Resnicks' walk hand in hand to the Synagogue. As they approach their destination, a familiar face walks toward them.

"Look Alex," whispers Mrs. Resnick. "It's that street thug who assaulted you some months ago. Let's turn around."

"Relax, my love. He's not going to do anything. At least not today with all these people walking the street. Now be quiet, he's getting closer."

James draws closer to the Resnicks'. He places his hoodie over his head, rubs his hands together, and smiles in the direction of the Resnicks'

"Good morning, sir and ma'am." He says in a sincere tone. "Have a blessed Sabbath."

"Shalom!" Replies Alex. "You have a great day too, young man."

"See Rita. I told you there was nothing to worry about. He's not a threat anymore. I bet Joseph is responsible for that boy's evolution."

"Maybe you're right." Replies Rita. "But I don't get why black men have to wear hoodies. It makes them look as if they're up to no good. I hate to say it, but he looks like a criminal."

"Well, he isn't a criminal. That's just a part of his culture he has embraced, as far as dress-wear is concerned. All right! Let's head inside and get ready for service."

The two of them head inside and are greeted with hugs and kisses from fellow members. Everyone is in a pleasant mood and looking forward to today's service.

A reading of the Torah is about to take place. The Resnicks' take a seat in the back, as they do not want to be a distraction. The reader raises the book over his head, causing the congregants to stand to their feet in tradition. When he is done reading, everyone takes their seats.

Rabbi Shapiro then steps up to offer his comments on the weekly scripture. Today's passage of scripture is taken from the book of Deuteronomy chapter 28, which deals with conditional blessings God placed on the Israelites.

"Brothers and sisters! Let us remember and always keep in mind that we are responsible for our success and our failures. This scripture teaches us that when we abide by the laws and statutes of God, we will never lack anything. But if God becomes displeased with our actions, destruction, terror, enslavement, and famine will surely come upon us. Let us always live a life that pleases our great Jehovah!"

The Rabbi continues his sermon on God's covenant with Israel. Although the message has dire consequences when God is displeased, there is a soothing joyous feeling knowing that God will bless his people greatly if they are obedient to him.

The congregants are feeling good about themselves, appreciating the Lord's graciousness to them.

The Rabbi completes his sermon and signals for the people to stand in prayer. As the members rise to their feet, BOOM! A loud thunderous sound rocks the walls of the Synagogue. The Rabbi and many others are jolted to the ground. Ten seconds later, a similar sound shakes the building again.

A ceiling chandelier falls right onto a woman, severely injuring her. Everyone is screaming and in a state of panic. They make a run for the main exit, but it appears as if something is blocking the door from the outside. Then a third and final KABOOM sounds off, causing part of the ceiling to collapse. Ceiling fans, light shades and other objects fall to the ground, injuring some and killing others.

Alex realizes that there isn't any way to get out of the room, so he takes his wife and pulls her into a corner of the room and crouch underneath a sturdy wood table.

The Rabbi is dead from the collapsed ceiling. Five children and eighteen adults die from this explosion. The fire and police department show up and do their best to locate survivors as well as bring out the

112

dead bodies. The Resnicks' survive, thanks to Alex's quick thinking. They were among the first to be rescued by the fire department. Mrs. Resnick is understandably shaken.

Three hours later, while still performing search and rescue, the NYPD determines that there were three pipe-bombs planted in three separate locations of the Synagogue.

Detective Flacco is on the scene, taking witnesses accounts and collecting all the video surveillance surrounding the building. He's bewildered at yet another terror attack.

"First the Church, now the Synagogue! Someone is targeting places of worship. But who?"

Meanwhile, the Jewish community is devastated by this terror attack. The street is full of mourners. Mothers lament for their children. Husbands grieve for the wives. Survivors have broken limbs and the eyes of others are permanently blinded.

Standing on the rooftop of a seven-story apartment building, adjacent to the Synagogue, is Krimion. Smiling from cheek to cheek, the rock-headed, self-righteous demon is again in admiration of his recent chaotic conquest. Now he eagerly waits to see if things play out as planned.

The next morning Detective Flacco is on the case, searching for clues for the culprit of the bombing. In his office, he goes through surveillance of the building from as early as the midnight before the blast. Skimming through the film, he doesn't find anything suspicious. That is until he gets to around three O'clock in the morning. In the video, he sees a young, dark-skinned man. The man is wearing a hoodie and

113

carrying a duffel bag, and is breaking into the Synagogue. And breaking in without much of an effort.

Detective Flacco zooms in to get a closer look at the guy. He then has a sketch artist draw a picture of the man to release to the public. Even with the camera zoomed in all the way, the artist doesn't have a distinct look at the guy. He draws his best of what the video displays, hands it to the detective, and has the drawing released to the media.

The detective then reaches out to the members of the Synagogue and asks if any of them can come in and watch the video. The Resnicks' are the first to come to the precinct.

The Resnicks' arrive, and are escorted to the detective's office. Right away, he shows them the video. Mrs. Resnick leans forward, takes off her glasses, and squints at the screen.

"Oh, my God." She yells. "That's that street thug. He goes to Joseph's church. He attacked my husband a few months back."

Alex then takes a closer look at the video

"That does look like him." He adds. "But the video isn't clear enough to tell for sure. Didn't we see him walking toward us from the Synagogue yesterday morning?"

"Yes, Alex. Yes we did cross paths yesterday."

"And look, guys, there's more," says the detective.

The detective then forwards the video to 11:03 AM; which is around the same time the Resnicks' were arriving.

114

"Mr. and Mrs. Resnick, here appears to be the same guy walking inside the synagogue. And five minutes later he is walking out. Unfortunately, his face is hidden by the hoodie covering his head."

"It's him! It's him! Screams Mrs. Resnick. I know it's him. He's a thug, a gangster, and an anti-Semite."

"Rita, you don't know that for sure. The video is blurry. His face isn't too visible."

"Alex, do you really think that it's a coincidence that we ran into him the same day, and now we have him on video."

"Rita, what we have is a video of a man who could be him."

"I can't believe you Alex. That's him, and you refuse to hold him accountable. Detective, that thug needs to be arrested."

"Alex, your wife is right. There's enough evidence to at least bring him in for questioning. And that's what I'm about to do right now. Do you guys know where he lives?"

"No," replies Mrs. Resnick. "But he goes to Pastor Johnson's church. He'll probably be there, if he hasn't already fled Brooklyn, that is."

The detective and the Resnicks' head over to FOC right away. When they get to the outside of the church, they can hear that Joseph is in the middle of his Sermon.

"Okay, Mr. and Mrs. Resnick. Here's the plan. We're going to find a seat in the back of the church. I need you two to keep your eyes open for the suspect. If you spot him, let me know immediately, and I'll

115

approach him after service. Whatever you do, do not draw attention to yourselves."

"Um, I think a white man with a badge, along with two old Jewish people all walking into a predominantly black church is attention all by itself." Jokes Alex.

"You're right about that," laughed the detective. "Just try and lay low. All right guys. Let's go in."

They open the front door and are now in the corridor of the church. Mrs. Resnick is getting anxious. They make their way to the sanctuary doors.

"All right, this is it." Says Alex.

Before they enter the church, the detective notices that Rita is a little jittery.

"Are you alright? Your hands are shaking."

Rita ignores him. She peeks through the stain glass windows of the doors. Meanwhile, inside the church, Joseph is talking about the bombing at the Synagogue. He asks that his congregation take up a collection for the synagogue, and the families of the victims.

"He's such a standup guy." Remarks Alex.

Mrs. Resnick is still jittery. Her body is boiled with frustration and rage.

She yells, "I can't take it anymore!"

She busts open the door and yells out something in her Yiddish tongue. All the members turn around in disbelief.

"Rita, calm down. What's the matter with you?" Says her husband.

Again Rita shouts out something in Yiddish.

From the pulpit, Joseph tries to interject.

"Mrs. Resnick, can you please speak English? Why are you disturbing our service?"

Rita then walks down the middle isles of the church. Alex tries to hold her back, but Rita presses her way down the aisle, pushing her husband out of the way. The detective scans the room for the suspect. Tears start to flow down the eyes of Rita.

"Which one of you thugs blew up my place of worship?"

"Whoa, wait a minute ma'am. What makes you think that one of my members would do such a thing?"

"Because my husband and I were just at the police station. We watched a video of a guy who attends this church, coming out of our temple, moments before the explosion. Alex, what's the guy's name again?"

Alex mutes himself.

"Alex, tell me his name, I said!"

"We don't need to say his name if he didn't do it."

"Oh, don't start that again. What is his name? Tell me his name!"

Alex is lost for words. He scratches his head and twiddles his fingers as he thinks of what next to say. His wife continues to annoy him for the name of the suspect.

"Stop wasting time, and tell everyone his name!"

"His name is James. James Desgranges!" Yells an unspotted voice within the pews of the church."

Rita and the detective look around.

"Who said that?" Shouts Rita.

"I said that. Me, James. James Desgranges." Says the young man, as he stands up. "I was at your Synagogue minutes before the explosion."

"I knew it! Shouts Rita. Detective, arrest this man!"

"Wait a minute, wait a minute. I said I was there, but I didn't say that I blew up the place."

"Then what were you doing there, exactly? Asks Rita. You certainly haven't converted to Judaism."

"No, I haven't converted. I was just curious about what the inside of a Jewish Temple looked like. I've never been to one before."

The detective walks up to James.

"Sir, would you mind coming to the precinct? You aren't under arrest. I wanna ask you a few questions."

"Oh hell no! So you want a black man to just voluntarily go to a place that was designed to keep him in bondage? How dumb do you think I am?"

118

"Well James, to be honest, we have a black man in a hoodie breaking into the Synagogue in the wee hours of the morning. And you look just like the guy in the video."

"Oh, so all black men look alike? I get it now."

"What I'm saying is that you are currently the prime suspect. And so James Desgranges, you are under arrest for the bombing of the mill basin Synagogue."

Detective Flacco attempts to handcuff James and reads him his rights.

James is deterrent.

"Get your hands off me! I thought you said you said that I wasn't under arrest!"

"Come on James. Let's not be difficult. Just comply and take a ride with me to the precinct."

"Hell no!" Says a defiant James, as he his flails his arms from the clutches of the detective.

Alex is torn.

"Do you have to arrest him? Don't you think that you need a little more evidence or eyewitness accounts?"

"I think I have all the evidence I need. Now, James, you can play nice and put your hands behind your back, or I can pull out my little Taser friend here, and have your body shiver from the effects of fifty-thousand volts. The choice is yours."

James immediately dashes away from the detective and makes a run to the exit. He pushes an usher out of his way while screaming,

"I didn't do it!'

He then barges through the corridor doors. Then, with extreme force, he pushes open the outside door. James takes two steps outside and is blinded by a whack across the head with a two-by-four. He's hit a second and third time for good measure.

James looks up and sees a swarm of Jewish men and women surrounding him. The detective then successfully places James under arrest.

"Now I can add resisting arrest to the list of criminal charges against you."

James can't believe what is happening to him.

"Who needs back-up when you've got your people on your side? Right, detective?"

The detective is a bit confused by the gang of Jews but says nothing except James' Miranda Rights.

Joseph, Willow, and many of the congregants run out of the building. They are upset by the treatment of one of their members.

"This is racial profiling," screams one of the members.

"That's' right. Just another case of being guilty while black" echoes another.

One of the Jews defends the arrest.

"Oh, stop with the race war. This man is as guilty as O.J. was, back in the 90s."

Tension starts to brew between both groups. Some of them are face to face with each other, debating the bombing. Men on both sides begin to tussle with each other. Krimion is there, and right on cue, he instigates with negative and upsetting whispers into the ears of the crowd.

"These black folks hate you Jews. They're jealous that God has blessed you with prosperity."

Not to be outdone, he goes over to the members of FOC and whispers in their ears.

"Those racist Jews are always getting away with corruption. And now they are getting away with framing James."

Not only is Krimion there, but so are fifty other demons that he has called to assist him. These demons were once beautiful angelic hosts in God's kingdom. Now, they are lowly, disfigured, unattractive demons, confined to the rule of Satan. These demons assist Krimion in inciting hatred into the minds of the two groups.

The Jews and black Americans are now all filled with hate through the words of Krimion and his helpers. But Krimion is not done. He picks up a rock from the ground and hurls it into the mob. The rock hits one of the Jews by the name of Jerry. Jerry, not knowing who threw the rock, throws a punch at the closest black person to him. The black man punches Jerry back, and the two of them wrestle to the ground.

Joseph is trying to calm everyone down, but it is too late for cooler heads to prevail. An all-out brawl has now begun among both groups.

Two Jewish men take a black man, and violently toss him onto a parked car.

Another black man takes a bamboo stick and slaps it over the back of a Jewish man.

Alex and Rita escape the brawl without injury. Seven police cars show up, and arrests are being made. There is no bias in the arrests, as both Jews and Gentiles are now in handcuffs.

Krimion is more than pleased with the latest outcome, but he is not done yet. Although many arrests are made, the two groups still outnumber the cops, and there are still several small squirms occurring. Joseph doesn't know what to do. He walks away from the melee, and into the street. He watches as blow after blow, kick after kick, and racial slur after racial slur is thrown from both sides of the fight. Both groups claim to be followers of God, yet they are both behaving like barbarians.

Joseph closes his eyes and starts praying for a miracle. He asks God to do whatever it takes to stop the fighting.

Then with his eyes still closed, and without much time for a reaction, a car backs up with great speed and blind-sides Joseph, knocking him to the ground. The car speeds away, with no one or no police cars in pursuit. The members of FOC rush over to their pastor.

"My back!" He cries in agony. "I can't move."

Willow rushes over to her husband. "Baby, are you hurt?"

"Yes! Call an ambulance."

Meanwhile, the gang of Jews scurry off to their homes and hiding places. Joseph is in excruciating pain. Willow has called 9-1-1, and the ambulance is on its way. Willow is freaking out, as she sits by her injured husband.

"You bastard! She yells. Whoever did this is going to pay."

"No, Willow. Be calm. I'll be alright. God will pronounce judgment in due time. Vengeance is the Lord's, not ours."

"No, Joseph, they must pay! Maybe God wants to use us to handle this battle. These people need to be taught a lesson. They need to suffer just as you are suffering."

Ten minutes later, and the ambulance is now on the scene. Two male EMT workers tend to Joseph. Joseph is flat on the floor and cannot move his lower extremities. The EMT workers cautiously place Joseph on their bed and wheel him into the ambulance. Willow whispers something to one of the church members, then hops in the ambulance to follow Joseph to the hospital.

Krimion watches with great pleasure, as he is now the author of this Mil Basin war.

"This is better than I thought." He says. "It's only a matter of time before Joseph gives up on God. And when that moment comes, I, Krimion, second in command to Satan, will kill Joseph once and for all and deliver him to my lord and master. Yes, Joseph. Things are just getting started. So for all the preaching you've done, for all the healing you've done, and for all the souls you have saved, it will all be for naught. Yes, Joseph. Your soul will be cast down into Hades. But I won't stop with just your soul; I will ensure that every last member of your despicable church will be in possession of Satan."

Krimion's Proposition
At the Resnicks'

"Rita, I have to ask you a question."

"Okay, what is it?"

"Come! Sit down in the living room. I need us both to be relaxed and comfortable."

"You're making me worried, Alex. Is there something wrong?"

"Well, that depends on your answer."

"Go on and ask, then."

"Okay Rita, I'm just gonna come right out and ask. Were you the one responsible for gathering almost every adult Jew in the neighborhood to Pastor Johnson's church?"

Rita walks away and mumbles something inaudible to Alex.

"Rita, look me in the eyes and answer me. Are you the one responsible or not? How did all those people know to come to Joseph's church on such short notice?"

"I don't know what you're talking about."

"Then look me in the eyes and say that it wasn't you. If you can look me in the eyes and deny involvement, I'll believe you. Now look me in the eyes and deny it."

Rita turns her head in the direction of her husband of 30 years. She can see that the events of today have troubled him deeply. Her mind then reflects to the day of the bombing. She recalls the fear that filled her heart. Her mind goes back to her wondering if that day was going to be her last day alive. She has flashbacks to the video of James coming out of the Synagogue just minutes before the bombing. As she comes out of her flashback, she loses whatever guilt and discomfort that was weighing on her conscious.

She gazes into the eyes of her husband.

125

"Yes! Yes, I texted as many people as possible to come to the church to make sure that James did not get away."

"I knew it! Rita, how could you be so stupid and impulsive? Look at the tension you've created. Why couldn't you just let the police do their job?"

"Do their job? Ha! It's a good thing our friends did show up. James almost got away."

Alex takes a book from off a nearby bookshelf and slams it on the floor.

"Rita, you idiot! We don't even know if James started the explosion. For all we know, that could have been just another person wearing a hoodie."

"I don't care if he did it or not. That guy deserves to rot in hell for the time he attacked you."

"But I've already forgiven him. Why can't you do the same?"

"Because, if you die, I have nothing. I have no siblings, no living aunts or uncles, and lastly, no children. God punished me several years ago when he made me miscarry my child. You would have thought that losing a baby would be punishment enough, but then God made me barren. Imagine that for all those years I couldn't get pregnant. We initially thought that you had a low sperm count, but the test came back negative on that. Then I went to my doctor, and the tests indicated that I had a damaged uterus. I'm supposed to be having grandchildren by now. Instead, I'm one incident away from being a widow. But I refuse to let that happen. If they attack us, we must attack them back. They assault my husband; then we hit them where it hurts the most."

"Hurts the most. What do you mean by that?"

"Nothing Alex. It's just an expression."

"No, no, no! You're implying something with that statement. Wait a minute. Are you also responsible for the fire at Joseph's church?"

Rita stands up. She strolls over to the living room window and gazes outside.

"Remember when our parents first moved to the states back in the 70's? The neighborhood was mostly safe from violence and looting. Slowly, black Americans and the black Caribbeans started moving in. Crime increased. Drug use became rampant. Drug dens in abandoned buildings. Crack bottles all over the floors. All this helped to devalue the real estate. Oh, and let's not forget the kids cutting school, and hanging out in malls and corner stores. But thanks to God, we got rid of most of these ingrates through eviction, foreclosure, and jail time. The wicked weed of the black community is not as great as before. But as I look at our community today, I see that things are regressing to the days of the 80s and 90s."

"Rita, I'm very disappointed with your position on the black community. Granted, some of the issues you mentioned are legitimate, but let's address a few of them right now. You brought up drug dens. How do you suppose crack, cocaine, and heroin got into black homes and not into ours? Someone or some group with higher power is the root of drugs penetrating the black neighborhoods. You mention crime. Well, Jewish people aren't a bunch of little angels either. Many of us commit acts that may not make the ten O'clock news but are just as

127

hideous as robbing and gang violence. Look at the temple we worship in. It was built off of dirty Russian mafia money. How about us as landlords when we turn off the hot water if our black tenants are a month or two behind in the rent. And you wanna talk about property value; I don't see black people getting drunk as sailors, pissing in public, on their most sacred religious holidays like some of us do. So spare me your racist and insensitive insults and answer my question. Are you in any way responsible for the fire at Joseph's church?"

"What do you think, Alex?"

"Don't answer a question with a question."

"Yes, Damnit! Yes, I started the fire. Well me and the Rabbi. May he rest in peace! The Rabbi and I started the fire in that God-forsaken place they call church! We were sick and tired of them bullying us around, devaluing our houses, and for me, it was a way to get even for James attacking you.

"Rita how could you do this! What happened to my sweet and loving wife? I feel like I don't know who you are anymore. You're a murderer now. Do you realize that?"

"I realize that we live in a kill or be killed world."

"So you've decided that because of one man's attack on me, an entire congregation should be punished. Now, look at what you've caused. Our temple was destroyed. Many are dead, including our Rabbi."

"And for this, Alex, there will be retaliation."

Alex is bewildered.

128

"Rita, I don't know what has happened to you, but I have to go for a drive. I pray that God opens up your heart and you repent of the evil you have done."

Alex leaves the house and gets into his car. He starts driving. The destination is unknown. He needs to clear his mind. Driving aimlessly for the next 17 minutes, he finally pulls over and parks his car.

"Oh shoot!" He blurts out loud. "I wonder how Joseph is doing."

He pulls out his phone and calls Joseph.

"Hi, Alex. This is Willow. We're at the hospital."

"Hi Willow. How is Joseph doing? Is he going to be all right?"

"It's not looking good. He has some spinal damage. He can't stand up. The doctors are running tests to see exactly what's wrong and what treatment to give."

"My God! I feel so bad. The things that happened today should have never happened."

"Yeah well it did happen, and Joseph seems to have received the brunt end of today's brawl."

"Can I come in and see him?"

"Sure, he's in room 301. We're at City hospital, on Carter Street."

"Okay, I'm heading there now."

Alex reaches the hospital twenty minutes later. He makes his way to the third floor. When he gets to Joseph's room, Willow is nowhere to be found. He opens the door and walks in.

129

"Hey, Pastor! It's me, Alex. Are you awake?"

A groggy Joseph turns his head slightly to the left and sees Alex.

"Yes' I'm awake. These pain medications have me sleepy though. Today was one hell of a day, huh?"

"That's an understatement, Joseph. It's been a crazy few months. I mean between your church fire, my temple bombing, and today's mob scene back at your church, I'd say that this experience is one for the ages."

"You ain't lying about that. But I can tell you this much, for some reason, the devil is at war with both of us. And when I say both of us, I'm referring to Christians and Jews. He is in the midst of all this contention. You're going to think that I'm crazy, but I recently came in contact with a demon. He is trying to create uneasiness in my marriage. God has been revealing things to me, but it is being revealed to me at a slower pace than normal. We can't let the devil win. But the best way to defeat the works of evil is by doing good.

"I don't think you're crazy at all. Jews also believe in the influences of demonic forces. Which leads me to this: I just became aware of the person who set your church on fire."

Just as that is being said, Willow approaches Joseph's room and overhears Alex's comment. She stands by the door, on the outside, so that she can continue to listen without being seen.

"Oh really, Alex? Tell me what you know."

"My wife and my now deceased Rabbi are the ones responsible for the fire."

"Oh is that so?" Says an irate Willow, as she charges into the room.

"Willow, please. You don't have to create a scene. Can you let the man finish?"

"No need to let him finish, Joseph. We need to call the cops, and have them arrest her."

"Wait a second there, Willow. Alex, how do you know that your wife and the Rabbi did this?"

"Because she told me. Based on some things she was telling me, I just had a feeling she was involved. It took some time to pry a confession out of her, but I finally got her to admit her guilt."

"There you have it! What more do we need? Time to call the police."

"No, Willow. That's not going to happen." Says Joseph.

"Huh! What do you mean that's not going to happen? You can't let her get away with this."

"I think I should forgive her."

"And why should we forgive her? Give me one good reason."

"I'll give you a good reason later. Now is not a good time."

"Well, I need to know now. Tell me!"

"Okay fine. I'll tell you. Alex, can you leave the room for a second?"

"No. let him stay."

"Willow, that isn't necessary."

"It's okay, Joseph. Being that he is your confidant and all, he might as well stay."

"Well since you're insisting, I'll tell you in front of Alex. We should forgive Rita for starting the fire because I am about to forgive you for cheating on me with Brian."

Willow stares at her husband in disbelief. Her mouth partially widens.

"Joseph, what are you talking about?"

"Don't play dumb with me now. I know that you two hooked up in the basement, the day of the fire."

In his discomfort, Alex tries to leave.

"Um, maybe I should go."

"Oh please, Alex. I need Willow to confess her sins before me right now. Come on Willow. Speak up! I've already overheard you talking to Brian on the phone. I heard you say that you felt like the fire was your fault. At first, I thought that you and Brian started the fire, but after eavesdropping on your conversation with him, him running out of the church, along with us now knowing that Rita and the Rabbi started the fire, I have determined that you and Brian were hooking up that day. It probably wasn't the first time either. Am I wrong, Willow?"

Willow stands there in front of her husband and Alex. Embarrassed that she's been caught, she drops to her knees and cries.

"I'm sorry, Joseph! I'm sorry. Yes, we've been having an affair for years. I still love you, Joseph. Please forgive me. Please!"

132

"Did you forget what I just told you a minute ago? I said that I am going to forgive you for cheating on me with Brian." This is why we're going to forgive Mrs. Resnick for what she has done. I will not report this to the authorities. Hopefully, they do not solve the case on their own."

"Thank you, Joseph. And since we're telling the truth, there's something else you need to know. Brian and I had sex during Willa's birthday party."

"You did what! You were screwing another man in my home?"

Willa falls to the floor sobbing, and she reflects on the reckless adulterous life she's been living for the past eight years. Joseph looks down on his wife and sees an embarrassed and scorned woman. He pities her, yet he's still in love with her. Despite all the lies and deceit, Joseph can't help but want to comfort his wife.

Joseph, I'm sorry. I'm so so sorry. You deserve better than this. You deserve a faithful wife. You deserve a virtuous woman. I am none of these things. Can you ever forgive me?

Stand up, Willow. It's okay. I forgive you. We're gonna work through this. It's gonna take some time, but I'm willing to fight for this marriage if you are.

"Yes, I'm willing. I'll do whatever it takes. Thank you, Joseph. I am going to make this up to you somehow."

"Okay, honey. We'll talk more when I recover."

"Well, I'm glad you two are able to try and work things out. So now that that is solved, where do we go from here concerning this beef between the black and Jewish communities?" Asks a concerned Alex. "The damage in the community has already been done."

"First, we have to put our trust in God. He will help us mend this community back together. Everything negative that is going on in our lives stems from demonic forces. We can defeat them if we are diligent in our pursuit of coexisting in peace."

"Joseph, I will gather up my people and try to persuade them to make peace. I am not sure if I should tell them about the demon you've seen. Most of us do not believe in the prophetic words of a Christian."

"As Alex finishes his statement, Joseph's eyes open wide like a window on a hot summer day. His head turns to the side facing his room door. He sees Krimion watching him from the hallway. Willow and Alex don't see the demon."

"What is it, Joseph? Asks an observant Willow."

"He's here."

"Who's here?"

"Krimion, the demon. He's watching us from the door window. Alex and Willow, I need you two to leave the room. It's time he and I have a little talk."

"Willow, are you sure that your husband isn't high off of too many pain meds?"

"Don't worry, Alex. I am completely sober, and I can see the demon as clear as I can see you and my wife. Now get out and stand by the door until I call for you."

Alex and Willow leave the room. Krimion enters. He's angry, annoyed, and determined.

As he enters the room, the ceiling to Joseph's room opens up. This is in the spirit realm and imperceptible to Joseph. A burst of fiery flames sent directly from God rush down from the ceiling and surround all four sides of Joseph's bed. Because of this fire, Krimion cannot get close enough to harm or possess Joseph. Krimion, therefore, stands about ten feet away from the fire barrier. He positions himself on the window sill, to the right of Joseph, and begins to speak.

"Your God has abandoned you. Your daughter is dead. Your church was set on fire. Your wife is an unfaithful whore. Now you're confined to this hospital bed as a paraplegic."

Joseph is not afraid and confronts his tormenting demon.

"Krimion, just like your father the devil, you speak lies. It is not me whom God has abandoned, but it is you when he threw you out of heaven years ago. And as for the current events of my life, this is no indication that God has forsaken me. This is all happening according to God's will."

"You're wrong, Joseph. It's over! You cannot win. Your church members are currently plotting revenge against the Jews. Your wife is even in on the plot. More blood will be shed at this rate. So rather than risking the loss of more lives, I have a proposal for you. You should give this some serious consideration. Give me your soul and I'll spare your people. Decline my offer and be assured that what you're experiencing now is just the tip of the iceberg."

"You demonic deceiver! I do not and will not ever negotiate with the enemies of God. I am not afraid of your attacks because though he slay me, yet will I trust him!"

Krimion momentarily scampers away from Joseph, hissing at Joseph, simultaneously. Joseph realizes what is bothering Krimion. He can't stand when someone recites bible verses at him. Joseph says another scripture.

"I shall not be afraid of the terror by night, nor the arrow that flieth at day. Nor the pestilence that walketh in darkness, nor for the destruction that wasteth at noonday. No evil shall befall thee, neither shall any plague come nigh thy dwelling."

Krimion covers his ears in disgust. The biblical words of truth cause pain and agony to flow through his immortal soul.

"Enough! He yells. One more word, and I'll make sure that you never walk again."

"You have no power over me, but it is I who has the power to tread on serpents. Today, you shall see the awesome power of God manifested through me."

Krimion lunges toward Joseph but is scorned by the invisible fire, and his body is jolted ten feet away. Joseph's confidence begins to grow when he realizes that Krimion cannot touch him.

Joseph then starts a short prayer.

"Father God in heaven, give me the strength to stand up and confront my enemy. Allow me to show him the power you can display through a mere man like me."

Joseph then hears the voice of God speak to him.

"Joseph, your prayer has been granted. Now rise up and defeat your enemy."

Joseph pulls his body in an upright position. Krimion's eyes are raised in disbelief. Alex and Willow, watching from the outside door, can see that Joseph is sitting up. They too are in shock. Joseph stands up on his feet and approaches Krimion. Krimion backs away due to the fire that is still around Joseph.

"No! No! This can't be. You're paralyzed. You shouldn't be walking this soon."

The flames of fire suddenly disappear, and Krimion makes his move. Quickly the demon rushes toward Joseph and grabs both of his arms. This is an unprecedented moment in time, where a human is literally wrestling with an evil spirit.

The two of them are locked hand in hand as they both try to outmuscle the other. Krimion releases his right hand from Joseph's left hand and thrusts his hand into the chest of Joseph. He is trying to pull Joseph's heart out of his body. Alex and Willow still only see Joseph. Alex considers going inside or calling for a nurse, but Willow stops him, assuring Alex that Joseph will be okay.

With Krimion's hand inside of Joseph's body and with a tight grip on Joseph's heart, Joseph starts to laugh.

"I see what you're trying to do, but there's one major problem, Krimion. My heart belongs to God!"

Joseph tries to pull Krimion's hand from his chest, but Krimion is relentless. But Joseph resiliency is frustrating Krimion.

137

"You're supposed to be paralyzed."

"And yet I'm not. This is the power of Christ. The anointed one. The one who was crucified, but is now risen from the dead. It is he who empowers me. It is he who has healed me. And now, I say to you, under the authority of Jesus Christ, get out of this place and go back to the depths of hell!

Joseph then throws Krimion against the wall, heart still in tack. Krimion makes one last desperate lunge at Joseph, but the fire that had left Joseph's body simultaneously reappears at the same time and scorches Krimion severely, and he is sent back to the presence of Satan.

With Krimion gone, Joseph signals for his wife and Alex to enter the room. At the same time, Joseph's doctor walks in and is shocked to see that Joseph is standing up.

"Mr. Johnson, how are you able to stand up like this? My x-rays indicate severe spinal damage."

Doctor, your x-rays weren't wrong at that time. But between then and now, my God has healed me. I prayed, and God answered."

"Is this for real?" The doctor asks. Maybe you weren't as hurt as we all thought. But whatever the case, I'm glad you're feeling better and appear to be healed, but I am gonna have to order another x-ray. I also should consult with some other doctors. We need to be sure that your miracle healing matches our tests."

"You do what you have to do, doc. I'll stay until you're comfortable enough to discharge me."

The doctor leaves the room and orders another x-ray. Joseph tells Willow and Alex everything that transpired between him and the demon. Because Joseph is standing on his two feet, completely healed, Alex believes everything Joseph's says about Krimion. Alex calls his cousin and orders a meeting with a small group of trusted fellow Jews. Joseph intends to do the same with his members once he is discharged.

Lucifer's Lower Level Losers

Location – Mauna Loa volcano, Hawaii

"Welcome back, Krimion. I see that you've been rebuked from Joseph's presence once again."

"My lord, the man is not afraid of demons. He conversed with me as if I was his equal."

"No, Krimion! That's where you're wrong. He conversed with you as if he had greater authority than you."

"His authority comes from God. There's nothing I can do about that, as long as his faith remains strong. He doesn't seem to give up on God."

"All men give up on God on at least a few occasions. It's simply up to you to catch them at that moment. But you can't catch them in the act if you're constantly getting cast out of their presence. I'm losing my patience with you, Krimion. You are making rookie mistakes. Mistakes that I can't even envision my lower level devils committing. I am now shortening the loose leash that I initially gave you. You are not as reliable as I once thought you were. A second in command does not get baited and fooled by a human. A second in command does not have a conversation with a mortal."

"Satan, my lord, my master. I assure you that I will not be cast away from Joseph again."

"Oh shut up, Krimion! I couldn't care less about your assurances or promises. Your mission with Joseph is getting shortened. You now have two weeks to bring him to me. If this doesn't happen, the hounds will be waiting for you."

"But Satan, why would you do this? I've been working hard to hand him to you. Yes, I've been cast away by him twice. But you need to give me more time to let my strategy play out."

Satan hovers over his subject. Krimion cowers to the ground. Fearful of what Satan might do.

"Don't you ever tell me what I need to do! Last time I checked, I was the lord of the underworld. And as powerful as you may be, don't ever suggest that you can give me orders. Now the reason why I am reducing your time is for the simple fact that every time Joseph casts you away, he gets spiritually stronger. He'll be almost godlike if he continues to exercise his powers on you."

"Satan, please. He begs. Sansar had much more time than I've been given. Although my plans have been met with setbacks, the result will be in our favor."

"Well the result better come within the next two weeks, or else your days in the hell-hole will be full of misery."

And with that, king Lucifer disappears from the presence of Krimion, as he's off to create his own reign of pain and agony among humans.

Krimion is enraged. He feels that Satan's lack of patience with him is unfair and unnecessary. Although he's had some pitfalls along the way, he has caused an enormous amount of damage in Joseph's life.

"Look at all the heartache I've caused. I have killed Willa, destroyed his church, and caused strife between his wife and his bastard's mother. The conflict between the blacks and the Jews is sure to linger on for a long time. Did Satan expect me not to have a hiccup here or there? We're not flawless demons ya know. Taking down a person like Joseph involves deliberate execution."

Now secretly listening in on Krimion's montage are five lower level demons by the names of Haracious, Mingro, Dexlan, Sarrus, and Santo. These five demons have lost their patience with Satan. They've regretted following him during the heavenly revolt. On several occasions they've gone back to God, asking for re-entry to heaven. But each time, God denies their plea. They know that their fate is for eternal damnation, but they want to make the best of their current situation and make hell on Earth as comfortable as possible.

"Sir Krimion!" Shouts Dexlan.

Krimion turns to the direction of the voices.

"Who's there?"

"It is I, Dexlan. Along with four others. We've come to talk to you."

"What do you want? I'm a busy devil, you know."

"Yes, we know this, Sir Krimion. We will leave you alone shortly. We couldn't help but overhear your semi-rant."

"Eavesdroppers, are we?"

"Oh no, sir." Answers Dexlan, with fear. "We would never do that. We understand that Satan is giving you a hard time in your quest to obtain the soul of Joseph Johnson."

"Yeah, and what is it to you?"

"We agree that two weeks isn't enough to accomplish this feat."

"It doesn't matter if you agree or not. If I don't deliver Joseph to Satan in two weeks, I'll be fed to the hounds."

"And that is why we're here. You see, Satan has been losing his patience with great frequency of late. He must have a sense that Jesus is returning soon to rapture his people and will put us into eternal death. Because every time one of us lower demons fail to satisfy his requirements as to how we handle the humans, he feeds one of us to the hounds."

"Three hundred and seven of us have been thrown to the hounds within the past sixty years." Adds Mingro. "I mean, how are we supposed to assist in human control, when at the slightest error, we are punished?"

"Okay guys, I get that Satan has been hard on all of us. He has an elevated vendetta against God. So to some degree, I can see why he would be short with patience. But with that being said, please tell me your purpose for coming to me. I need to get back to preparation for Joseph."

Haracious steps up to Krimion bends to one knee and lowers his head. "Lord Krimion, live forever!"

Krimion is taken aback.

"What is this supposed to mean?"

"You see, my lord, we have been taking a pulse of the demons down here. A majority of us are infuriated with Satan. He is reckless and out of control. We feel that now is the time to stand to up him and take over his kingdom."

"Do you fools honestly believe that you can take this kingdom away from Satan? Only God can do that. Besides, this is treason. If Satan found out that you all were planning a revolt against him, he would do something to you all far worse than to feed you to the hounds."

"That's why we've only told a select few of our plans. Lord Krimion, we've watched you through the years as you have brought countless souls to Satan. We believe that you have rightfully earned your way as Satan's number two. But we also believe that you would make an even more superior leader. We are asking you, oh great Krimion, to be our King and lead us into a revolt against Satan."

Krimion folds his arms and paces left to right across the five demons. He's in deep thought, carefully considering this revolutionary pitch.

"So let me get this straight. You want me to lead you in a takeover of hell? I highly doubt that I would go through with such an idiotic plan, but tell me, how would this so-called revolt work?"

"We would go to war," answers Haracious.

"And how do you plan on winning this war, Haracious?"

"That's where we would lean on your expertise. We are asking you to devise a plan that would help us defeat Satan and anyone who aligns themselves with him."

"You guys are something else. Don't you know that a revolt would require the recruitment of more demons? Some of them could turn out to be spies and informants to Satan. No, no. It's too risky and too costly. When I succeed with my Joseph mission, I will be granted great authority by Satan. Perhaps once in authority, I can have some influence on his dealings toward you guys. Satan's intelligence is far beyond our comprehension. This revolt is a bad idea. It would only lead to the absolute destruction of those opposing our leader. Now the five of you need to forget about this takeover attempt and learn to deal with Satan as he is."

"But Lord Krimion, interjects Santo.

"Don't Lord Krimion me. This discussion is over! Now get out of my face before I personally throw you all to the hounds."

"Yes, my lord. As you wish," answer the five demons.

The demons walk away from Krimion, saddened that their pitch to Krimion was rejected. Meanwhile, unbeknownst to Krimion, Satan was lurking in a corner area of his lair. He was listening in on the entire conversation between Krimion and the five demons.

"Hmm. Maybe I have been a tad bit hard on Krimion. Perhaps I was a bit hasty in reducing his time with Joseph. He is my most loyal, committed, and thorough devil. Krimion kind of reminds me of myself when I was under the tutelage of Jehovah. Krimion would always seek my counsel and pick my brain about things I have learned. His desire to get better is only second to me. So for him to refuse a revolt displays class and loyalty. If he fails to bring me Joseph after two weeks, I'll grant him a four-month extension. But I won't tell him of this now, lest he becomes complacent.

Tragic Reconciliation

145

It's a week later, and tension between the Jews and blacks has now reached its climax. Fights between the two groups started over the simplest of reasons. One fight occurred when a good-natured, well-intended Jewish man modestly said good morning to a black male. The black male took offense at the guy's pleasantry and assaulted him. On another occasion, a Jewish man attacked a black man inside of a supermarket just because he thought that the black man had cut him off at the check-out line. And the verbal attacks on social media coming from both sides were a shame to those who call themselves children of God.

And the media was loving every minute of the turmoil. In some instances, it was them who riled up one group against the other.

But after a week of brawling, Joseph and Alex were able to convince the two sides to gather together in one place and talk things over. They all agreed to have the meeting at the Opera House, on Grand Avenue. Ironically, the Opera House is owned by a black woman and a Jewish man.

So today, members of the community are filing in one by one for the meeting. Police presence can be felt within a five-block radius of the Opera House. To avoid conflict, the black Americans were asked to enter the building on the east-side entrance, while the Jews are requested to come in through the west-side. The last thing Joseph and Alex wanted is another physical altercation. Everyone had to go through metal detectors. If any weapon is found on a person, he or she would be detained and possibly arrested.

The Opera House seats 3000 guests, and the room is filled to capacity. The scene is likened to that of the United States Presidential

State of the Union Address; where Democrats sit on the left side of the room, while Republicans sit on the right. Coincidentally, the Jews are sitting on the left side, and the black Americans are sitting on the right.

Prayers for a successful meeting are done back-stage by Alex and Joseph. The two of them come out to center-stage together. They had choreographed an all-in-one, alternating opening speech. They are ready to commence today's meeting. Joseph starts first.

"Good evening, ladies and gentlemen! Today, we come together in the name of peace. We come together in the name of Jehovah-Shalom."

"That's right, Joseph. We come together in the name of the Prince of Peace."

"Yes, Alex! Whether you are Jew or Gentile, black or white, Muslim or atheist, peace among our brethren is the only thing that matters." Over the past several days, we've been at each other's throats. And for what? Simply over a misunderstanding."

"Nah, this ain't no misunderstanding!" Yells the recently released James Desgranges.

The police had determined that he was not the culprit behind the Synagogue bombing. That investigation is still on-going.

James stands up and looks at Alex.

"A few months ago you spat on me as I walked past you and your wife. You claim that it was an accident, but I don't believe you."

Joseph tries to interject.

"Now, now. We're not here to talk about the past."

147

"No Joseph. It's okay. Let me address James' accusation."

Alex's old body jumps off the stage and walks over to James. The two of them are just four feet away from each other.

"James, when you look at me, what do you see?"

"Ha! I don't think that you want me to answer that question."

"You're funny James. But the question is more rhetorical than literal. You see, I'm a 65-year-old man. I'm five feet ten, and 168 pounds, soaking wet. I graduated from NYU with a major in business and a minor in psychology. James, I can assure you that I did not deliberately try to spit on you. And look at me compared to you. What are you, 6'3, 210 pounds?"

"Actually, I'm 6'4, 215 pounds. But who's counting?"

"Ah! You're even bigger than I thought. Now let me tell you this. We Jews have developed a reputation over the years for many things, but one thing I can tell you about myself and most other Jews is that we're not stupid. We may be cheap, but definitely not stupid."

The crowd chuckles at Alex's references to Jews being thought of as cheap. Joseph laughs as well, and Alex wipes his forehead off in comedic relief.

"You know I was a bit worried about that joke. I've been practicing it on Joseph for days; wondering if I'd get a good reaction or not. So let me quit while I'm ahead and get back to my point. James, I have too much respect for humans to spit on anyone intentionally. As God as my witness, the wind blew that spit on you. Nevertheless, I apologize."

James takes two steps toward Alex. Fellow Jews stand up in anticipation of an attack.

"No worries, fellas. I just wanted to tell Alex that I am sorry for assaulting him that day, and I am asking for his forgiveness."

"Of course I forgive you. I was over that incident a long time ago."

James then embraces Alex with a hug. The crowd applauds the reconciliation.

Joseph speaks.

"Ladies and gentlemen! Today is a good day. It is a day ordained by God to bring peace to his people. Forgiveness is a good first step, but we must be aware of the adversary."

"What adversary?" Shouts a Jew in the audience.

"I will explain. As most of you recall, I was run over by a car, and temporarily paralyzed. Confined to my hospital bed, I was in the spirit when a demon confronted me. He is the one who has been tempting us with hate. The same way Satan tempted Eve to eat the forbidden fruit, is the same way he tempted Cain to kill Abel. Today he is tempting us with hate, envy, wrath, and jealousy. Yes ladies and gentlemen, the Adversary, otherwise known as Satan, has dispatched a demon to torment me and try and take my soul. I lost my daughter, I almost lost my marriage, and my church was set on fire. But every time it seemed like I was cursed, I refused to blame God. I refused to turn my back on him. My faith in God has angered the demon. Twice I have seen him and twice I have rebuked him from my presence. But he is relentless. And I fear that he and other demons will

149

be back on the prowl. This is why we must continue to pray, and ask God to watch and protect us. Brothers and sisters, evil is always around. It is lurking at the doors of our hearts. You have heard it said that we must overcome evil with good; but today I say, let's overcome evil with God."

The entire congregation rises to their feet. Responses of amen and applauses ring through the crowd. They concur with Joseph's plea.

Alex gets back on the microphone and shouts, "Today we will be known as God First Community. Whether it is the God of the Old Testament, New Testament, Koran, or any other religion or non-religion, if we follow the moral values of our beliefs, evil will not prevail."

Alex and Joseph then allow those in attendance to speak their mind and express how they can make their community a more respectful and peaceful place to live. The consensus is that both groups can coexist in peace and harmony.

A gentleman in the back of the room wearing a gray blazer and black pants is not impressed with the moment of solace.

"Well, why don't we all just hold hands and sing kumbaya! You guys are something else. No matter how nice and kind we all agree to be, it does not change the fact that some of you Jews in here are money hungry, self-righteous, tax evading, welfare stealing criminals. We can all try to act nice to each other, but in a week or two, things will go back to normal."

"Please, sir. No need for name calling and casting judgment. Now as for your point about things going back to the way it was, Alex and I will be spear-heading an annual day of events. The day will consist of softball, flag football, volleyball, and other activities. All games will be comprised of mixed teams. This is just one of many ways for us to get to know each other. But as for your comments as it pertains to Jews, please do not stereotype anyone in here. I'm sure you wouldn't like it if a Jew in here referred to black people as lazy-section-8-having-ignorant bastards. And thirdly, I can tell your comments are not of yourself, but that of an evil spirit, speaking to you, riling you up with anger. This is what I am warning us all to be aware of."

Joseph is right about the evil spirit. Krimion had sent another demon to stir things up at the meeting. This devil has one of the softest and seductive voices in all of hell. The demon is known for turning people into serial killers. In heaven, his name was Zordain, but Satan re-named him Silky. One of his greatest gifts is the ability to avoid detection from spiritually alert humans like Joseph. Joseph could not see the spirit, but he could tell that the man wasn't himself.

"Yeah right!" Shouts the man. "There's no evil spirit in this place. You're just playing mind games on us to get us to live in peace with the Jews. But the fact remains that they don't like us and we don't like them!"

Groans and moans fill the room, as the once synchronized mixed multitude are bothered by the strange man's comments.

Another black man, by the name of Gary, stands to his feet and walks over to a random male Jew and holds his hands.

"This is my brother," he says. "He is my brother because he bleeds the same color as you and I. So if you have a problem with him, then you have a problem with me. And if you're not going to try and live in peace with us, then I suggest you move to another neighborhood!"

151

The entire congregation affirms Gary's rebuke by demanding that the man either shut-up or leave the room.

The disgruntled man leaves the room and goes on his way. Talks reconvene for an additional fifteen minutes before the meeting ends. Alex and Joseph are more than pleased with the outcome of today's session.

As everyone heads outside to go home, numerous news reporters are out interviewing the participants of the meeting. Positive reports are expressed to the media, minus the altercation with the enraged strange black man.

Willow, Alex, and Joseph are all standing at the front doors shaking hands of those who were in attendance. As the attendees depart, Jews and blacks can be seen conversing with each other. Many of them realize that they have similar interests in things like sports, fishing, T.V. shows, and movies.

While the outdoor fellowship is going on, the strange black man walks back toward Alex, Joseph, and Willow. Silky, the soft-spoken demon, is beside him. Joseph senses that something is afoot in the area. He can't quite tell what it is exactly, as the strange black man cannot yet be seen among the crowd.

Joseph's spiritual radar heightens.

"Alex, Willow. Everybody needs to go home now."

Alex is confused.

"Why, what's wrong?" "Everyone is having a good time."

"Yes, but something is about to go down. I just can't tell what that something is."

Willow now sees the strange black man approaching. His face is intensified with rage. Willow can see the man reach into the left inner-pocket of his blazer. As he reaches for his pocket, he fixes his eyes on Alex. Willow grabs Joseph.

"Joseph, look. Watch out!"

The man pulls out a gun and aims it at Alex. Joseph sees this and steps in front of Alex. Immediately, Willow jumps in front of Joseph.

Bang! The gun goes off. Alex, Joseph, and Willow all fall to the ground. The bullet struck Willow in the back. The strange man is immediately subdued by the crowd.

Joseph clutches onto Willow, as they lay on the floor.

"No! He cries. "No, not again!"

Willow is lifeless. Voiceless, if you will. Not even a bellow of pain emits from her mouth. Her eyes are wide open, with blood draining out of her back. Her breathing stops and her heart loses its beat.

Joseph realizes that his wife is dead.

"Lord Jesus, why? Why did you let this happen? My wife is gone. My wife is gone!"

The strange man is getting beat up severely by the Jews and blacks. Joseph's doesn't have a care as to what they do to him. All he knows is that his wife is dead.

Krimion stands before Joseph, but Joseph cannot see him, as he is too emotionally exhausted to be spiritually aware of his surroundings. Krimion starts to speak to Joseph but makes it seem like Joseph hears his thoughts.

"Look at your life. Look at yourself. Your daughter, dead! Your wife, dead! Everything God promised you has turned out to be a lie."

The fire that surrounded Joseph while he was in the hospital is not protecting him now. Krimion cautiously draws closer to Joseph.

"Your life has no meaning. It's time to end this misery.

In haste, Joseph gets up off the floor and takes the handgun away from the strange man. Alex and others think he is going to shoot the murderer. Instead, he turns the gun to himself, aims at his heart.

Nooo! Screams Alex, as he lunges toward Joseph. Joseph pulls the trigger simultaneous to Alex jumping on him.

Joseph is shot.

Mauna Loa volcano - Hawaii

"My Lord."

"Yes, Krimion."

"It is finished. Joseph Johnson is as good as yours."

"Well, I don't see him here. Where is Joseph's soul? Show me, Joseph."

"He isn't dead, yet. But he might as well be. He tried to commit suicide. He almost did, but that blasted Jew friend of his, Alex, intervened and caused the gunshot to hit his shoulder instead of his heart."

"Oh, so you failed to kill him."

"Yes, but he's gone mad. He's currently locked up in a psychiatric hospital. He's not himself at all. Totally under the control of my minions. The doctors have him in a straight-jacket, but as soon as the opportunity is given, we will make sure that he kills himself."

"Well I suppose I owe you a pat on the back, or a job well done, to reward you for perseverance in bringing down Joseph. To reward you for the job well done, I am officially naming you my Chief Lieutenant."

"Thank you, my lord. I am truly honored to be elevated to this position. You will not regret this, my king."

"Good! Now go back to Joseph and ensure that he doesn't get delivered."

155

"Yes, master. I will go back to Joseph momentarily. But before I go, there is something that you need to know."

"And what is that?"

"A large portion of your followers are planning a revolt against you. They are looking for new leadership and have asked me to lead them to war against you. I rejected their proposition and advised them to rethink their idiotic idea. However, I have just learned that they are…."

"On our way." Interrupts a battle-ready Domingo, as he, along with half of Satan's kingdom has now appeared before Satan and Krimion. They were all hiding beneath rocks, doors and anywhere possible, waiting for the right time to attack.

Krimion stands in front of Satan, remaining loyal to his master.

"Step aside, Krimion. I haven't had an all-out battle in a very long time. Let me show you how to defeat an army single-handedly."

Satan approaches his betrayers. Each of them armed with spears and ready to dethrone their former leader. With spears in hand, the revolters form a semi-circle around Satan. The circle is not just at eye level. Thousands of demons elevate three stories above ground in an attempt to keep Satan from flying away. Satan attacks the front-line of the revolters by sweep-kicking them out of the way. Still, the semi-circle is mostly intact.

They draw closer to Satan, causing him to retreat his steps. Unaware of where he is, Satan backs up closer to the gates of the hounds. Krimion is right behind Satan, making him even closer to the hounds.

Satan attempts another foot sweep at his aggressors. The ones who are not attacked immediately spear Satan around his body. For the first time since his heavenly revolt, he looks defeated. The revolters push Satan within two feet from the gate. All hope for the prince of darkness appears to be lost.

Krimion steps in front of Satan.

"Don't worry, my master, I'll defeat these defiers for you."

Krimion spots a long twenty feet chain that is laying on the ground to his right. He takes the chain and whips it around several times in lasso-like fashion. He's about to hit the revolters with the chain, but instead, he whips Satan by his two feet, tying them together.

"What are you doing, you buffoon!"

"Sorry Satan, but your reign in this underworld is over."

"How dare you double-cross me? Release me at once!"

"No, Satan! It's time to give you a taste of your own medicine. Domingo, open the gate to the hounds."

"What? No, Krimion. Don't do this!"

Domingo quickly opens the gate. He and every last revolting demon, Krimion included, is pushing Satan to the hounds. Satan tries to out-muscle them, but he is outnumbered and cannot withstand their combined strengths. The demons quickly dump Satan into the dungeon of hounds. They shut and lock the gate, and listen for the sounds of the hounds gnawing at their former king.

Everyone is silent. Dexlan is confused.

157

"I don't hear anything."

"Me either." Adds Sarrus.

Satan is at the gate walls, and he begins to speak through the walls.

"Ever heard the phrase, don't bite the hand that feeds you? Did you guys really think that my hounds would ever feast of the one who provides their meals? You guys are dumber than I thought. Also, I was pretty much playing possum with you all. Even with your combined strengths, you're not as powerful as I am. Lastly, to my friend Krimion, I was always aware of your betrayal. Remember, no one is as great at deception than I am. I knew those fools were plotting against me before they ever came to you."

"Now we can resolve this matter in one of two ways. One, you can open the door, let me out, and your punishment will not be too severe. Or two, don't open the door, allow me to use unnecessary energy to open the door, and your punishment will be that of one beyond the realm of your limited comprehension. The choice is yours. I'll give you a few minutes to think this through."

Meanwhile, back in the human realm, Joseph is in the psychiatric ward of Saint Mark's hospital. Fast asleep and heavily medicated, Jesus visits him in his sleep through a vision.

Jesus takes Joseph in an outer-body experience. His spirit leaves his body and is taken miles into the clouds of the air.

"Joseph, my son. You've been through a lot. You have suffered great losses."

"Jesus, please. Please tell me why all of this is happening to me. Why have you allowed me to experience such great tragedies?"

"To make you stronger, Joseph."

"Stronger? How can I gain strength from this? I have lost my mind, and have been locked away in a nut house. What purpose is my life serving? I can't take another loss. I lost my one and only daughter, and now I've lost my wife.

"Well, I'm glad you brought that up. You are not the biological father for Willa. Brian Gimber is the father. Willow and Brian have been keeping this secret from you all this time. I was giving Willow time to confess this to you, but she never did. So I allowed her life to be taken away."

"I can't believe that the one woman I decide to marry turned out to be an adultering whore. Still, I loved her. It seems like every woman I get strong feelings for, I lose, one way or the other. You know what? I'm done. Please, Lord, do me a favor. Take me out of this world, and into your kingdom."

"So you want to die, Joseph? Is that what you're saying? I could do that, but that would just anger Satan, and he would go after Favor."

"My son?"

"Yes, your son. The minute Satan realizes that your soul is not with him, he will come after your son in retaliation. I should point out that I have anointed Favor for ministry as well. His calling won't come to fruition until he's in his teen years. But Satan will create chaos and hardship in Favor's life if you depart from this life and into my kingdom.

So the choice is yours. Leave the earthly realm and come with me into paradise, understanding that demonic forces will attempt to torment your only son, or stay alive and help Favor fight off the spiritual wicked works of the prince of darkness. But before you make your decision, let's go back to the psych ward. There's something you need to see."

Joseph and Jesus head back to Joseph's room in the psych ward. Joseph is still in the spirit and can see his lifeless body lay on the bed. But in the room, standing over his body, are Karen and Favor. Favor is praying to God for the deliverance of his dad.

"Please God, wake up my daddy. Make him better. Make him normal. I want him to go home. Please bring back my daddy. Please, God."

Jesus looks at Joseph.

"So Joseph, the answer to your son's prayers lies within whatever decision you make. It's decision time. What's it gonna be? But make your decision soon. The fate of many is contingent on what you do right now; even the fate of Satan. So, is it going to be, eternal life with your Savior or temporal life with your Favor?"

www.ingramcontent.com/pod-product-compliance
Lightning Source LLC
Chambersburg PA
CBHW051831170626
46807CB00003B/1127